Wifeshopping

Steven Wingate

Wifeshopping

 STORIES

A Mariner Original • *Houghton Mifflin Company*

BOSTON   NEW YORK   2008

For information about permission to reproduce selections from
this book, write to Permissions, Houghton Mifflin Company,
215 Park Avenue South, New York, New York 10003.

www.houghtonmifflinbooks.com

Library of Congress Cataloging-in-Publication Data
Wingate, Steven.
　Wifeshopping : stories / Steven Wingate.
　　p. cm.
"A Mariner original."
　ISBN 978-0-547-05365-3
　1. Mate selection — Fiction. I. Title.
　PS3623.I6623W54 2008
　813'.6 — dc22　　　　　　　2008004733

Book design by Melissa Lotfy

Printed in the United States of America

EB-L　10　9　8　7　6　5　4　3　2

"Beaching It" won the 2006 Gulf Coast Prize in fiction and was first published
　in volume 19, no. 1 (Winter 2006–07).
"Me and Paul" won the 2006 Fiction Prize from the *Journal* and appeared in
　volume 30, no. 1 (Autumn/Winter 2006).
"The Balkan House" was a finalist for the 2006 Mississippi Review Prize in
　fiction and appeared in volume 34, nos. 1 and 2 (June 2006).
"Inside the Hole" was first published in the *Open Windows 3* anthology from
　Ghost Road Press (Spring 2008).
"A Story about Two Prisoners" was first published in *Quarter After Eight,* vol-
　ume 3 (1996) and reprinted in *Matter,* no. 7 (Winter 2005).
"Meeting Grace" was first published in *River City* (University of Memphis),
　volume 25, no. 2 (Fall 2005).
"Three A.M. Ambulance Driver" was first published in *Green Hills Literary
　Lantern* (Truman State University), no. 17 (Spring 2006).
"Our Last Garage Sale" was first published in the *Pinch* (University of Mem-
　phis), volume 27, no. 2 (Fall 2007).

Contents

Foreword

EACH OF THE THIRTEEN stories in this collection turns on a defining moment between a man and his fiancée—or a woman he could imagine as his intended. The lovers in these stories are set to find The Flaw, the excuse to back out, to tear down the picture of a life together. The title suggests that these decisions fall to the men, but the women walk too.

What makes these studies in discovery and disillusionment so startling and affecting is the energy of Steven Wingate's language, and the agency of his characters. The author's stance ensures a fair fight: in a *Wifeshopping* story, both parties have a chance.

While making love to a married woman on a beach in Rockport, the man in "Beaching It" wonders whom he would marry if God held a gun to his head and gave him thirty seconds to choose. He remembers a twenty-year-old waitress in Texas: "Those eyes looked like they could let an awful lot of my behavior slide, if I'd just let hers slide too. If you can forgive each other like that, then there's no use doing anything you'd need to forgive each other for . . ."

In "Three A.M. Ambulance Driver," a motivational speaker sizes up a female EMT in a diner and thinks, "She could be the one. I could make her the one. I could make a thousand women like her the one." She offers a raw reality check to his stagey narcissism.

In "Bill," an affianced couple go to a flea market in New England, where they meet a doctor selling his clothes. The young man buys a load of them. The defining moment comes when the doctor offers an outfit for the young woman—an outdated ensemble belonging to his dying wife.

Grace is the narrator's demonic sister in "Meeting Grace," the account of escalating emotional abuse at a dinner to introduce sister and fiancée. The sister taunts the fiancée, adding ominously, "He's going to turn into his father one day . . . He'll tell you who you can be and who you can't be." The narrator's fiancée, a serene woman from India, is rendered such that her attempt to understand is excruciating. "I had no idea what they did with crazy people in India," the helpless narrator realizes. It is a story about fear that makes what it fears happen.

And when the woman is the one who suddenly sees what life would be like if she goes forward into marriage? "In Flagstaff" closes this cohesive collection with a couple at the funeral of the man's uncle. The man's condescension to the locals prompts the following: "Bethany wanted to see a war between the pompous creeps and the real people, and she wanted to be the one who started it." And before exacting a voluptuous revenge, she finds that "marrying Nolan felt like . . . taking everything she believed she could be and throwing it down a sewer just to prove she had control over her decisions." This story ends not in anger, but in a confluence of vision, freedom, and possibility, written with eloquence and insight.

There is a thrilling moment in the story "Faster" that comes when a man on a treadmill feels he cannot change any more by shedding his skin, but must outrun it, so to speak, while it is still on his body. "So he kept on jabbing at the pace button, going up past ten miles an hour where he'd never been before. The treadmill underneath him moved so fast he couldn't tell his feet apart, didn't know which arm to swing next. But he didn't fall, and started to feel like he'd never fall, and right then he felt the first pieces of skin pull away from his body like old paint flecking off in the wind."

The stories in *Wifeshopping* expand with subsequent readings; they do not end on the page, but continue in a reader's mind. Their success comes from Wingate's surpassing skill as a writer, and his vision of what can happen when we are made to forfeit a fantasy.

AMY HEMPEL, November 2007

Wifeshopping

Beaching It

EVERY GUY I KNOW who's even the least bit footloose has the same fantasy as me — you buy a junker, point it someplace you never ever heard of, and drive it till it dies. Till it breaks down in the middle of the night with nobody around to help you, and you wake up the next morning with your engine all over the road. A couple miles away there's some dinky little town that's too small for your atlas, and even though the folks there can't help you with your car, they're nicer to you than anybody else you ever bumped into. You hang around for the vibe and soon enough you run into the perfect girl for you, the soulmate you stopped believing was out there. Then all these squishy feelings come out. You start thinking about baby names, and you laugh at yourself for ever wanting to run away from the daddy you were supposed to turn into all along. You look around at all the great things you've got in this little nowhere town and decide that being yourself isn't so bad after all, decide to pitch your tent there and watch your hair go gray.

For a while I thought maybe Rockport, Massachusetts, was going to be that place for me. And even though I didn't break down there, I did get to town by accident. This guy Jacob, a glassblower I've been running into on the circuit for years, fell in love with some girl in South Carolina and decided to stay there instead of coming up to Rockport like he usually does in the summer. He'd rented out a storefront in their little shopping district the last three seasons in a row, and asked me to take his spot this summer so he could keep his options open for next year—just in case the Carolina girl didn't work out. It was a gamble to take Jacob's offer, since I usually made good money at the summer craft fairs around D.C., but it turned out the New England types went nuts for me. I've got an antique metalsmith's forge—a little one that fits in the back of my van—and I mostly make old-fashioned-looking candelabras. When the summer shoppers saw me with my leather apron and my ponytail, they said I looked just like Paul Revere. Then they gave me their money and I said, "God bless," like a good, patriotic American. I made more cash my first six weeks in Rockport than the past two summers down in D.C. combined.

I had a woman there too, Mrs. Beverly Lillie, who wasn't my soulmate but at least she kept me happy and bought me dinner. Her husband was some hot-shot investment banker who kept a condo and another woman down in Boston, and Bev didn't seem to mind spending his money on me. She was making her rounds on that first Saturday in August, waving to me as she bounced up the road, but then she stopped to chat with her friend Julie at the doll shop. I barely watched her because I was busy wrapping up the six candelabras that Mrs. Kashgarian hired me to make for her daughter's bridesmaids.

"You sure they're not too heavy, Mrs. K?" I taped down the tissue paper and slid everything into the canvas bags I got from Bev. They had the logo of her husband's company on the front, big and orange. "They're iron, remember?"

"Don't think I'm that old, Mr. B." She loved me because I was half-Armenian, like her daughter. She'd guessed it the first time she saw my face—which surprised me, because the only thing about me that sticks out as Armenian is my name, Bedrosian—

and I was her pet from then on. Her daughter down in Boston was marrying another half-Armenian, and I guess the candelabras were old-country enough as long as somebody with Armenian blood made them. She wanted to see me settled down with a nice half-Armenian girl myself, and had great things to say about one of her daughter's bridesmaids. I checked the bags to make sure they'd hold up okay.

"I just don't want your arms to get tired carrying them," I said, holding out the bags for Mrs. K. I watched Bev stroll up the road, sidestepping a family of tourists who were cramming saltwater taffy down each other's throats and laughing. "I know you've got a lot of work to do with the wedding."

"You keep smiling." She winked and took both bags, then squared her shoulders for the walk to her car. "Somebody'll notice you."

By then Bev was standing right behind her, cracking a smile at me for flirting with an old lady. My eyes must've gone to hers, because Mrs. K turned around to see who I was looking at. From the way her nose scrunched down, I could tell that a blonde pushing forty and still showing off her cleavage was not the kind of woman she wanted noticing me.

Mrs. K said, "Excuse me," then walked off with a grunt. I'm sure she blamed my non-Armenian half for the kind of women I slept with.

"Is that your Romanian lady?" Bev was wearing my favorite sundress, the blue-and-pink striped one that showed off her great collarbones. She had that tight, freckly skin you see on lots of New England beach women, especially the ones who don't wear makeup, and thick blond hair that always smelled like salt. That felt like it had tiny little grains of salt in it, left over from the wind.

"Armenian, please. Yeah, four hundred dollars worth."

"Good." She turned to look at Mrs. K, who was already lost in the crowd. "Then you can take *me* to dinner sometime."

"Tonight?"

"No, not tonight. I want to beach it tonight."

"All right. See you there, then."

Bev looked sideways to check if anybody was watching, then blew me a little kiss. "Keep smiling," she whispered. "Somebody'll notice you."

Then she went back to visiting her buddies, and I went back to playing Paul Revere. Bev never gave me anything more than a wink or a long-distance kiss in public except when we were at her favorite restaurant, Orry's, a dive for rich snots who still wished it was twenty years ago. Everybody there hated her husband, and wouldn't stop to pick him up if he was bleeding to death by the roadside — he was suing everybody in sight over a building permit, some shit like that. You could tell half the regulars were waiting for their chance at her, even if it meant cheating on their wives. They knew I was Bev's squeeze, which I guess meant I was helping them get back at Jeffrey Lillie somehow, so they acted like my friends as long as she was sitting next to me. Sometimes before she even got there, if they knew she was coming by later. If she wasn't, they looked at me like I was a garbageman.

At sundown I moved the goods inside and put up my BACK TOMORROW! sign, then took a shower and a quick nap in the back room. I was starving but didn't want to eat too much, because Bev never ate at all when she got horny — like she was a wrestler who had to be at the perfect weight before a match. I wondered how she got that way, if it had anything to do with ovulating and if women can still feel their eggs drop after their tubes are tied. But I couldn't figure it out. Then I dreamed about Bev and Mrs. K getting into a catfight over me, but it could've been part fantasy too. Mrs. K was a tough old bat, and wouldn't give up even though Bev had her pinned down and was tearing her hair out.

One of them started making weird sounds, which turned out to be a real live kid outside my window playing a kazoo. I got up, put on some cologne Bev gave me, and headed down to Orry's for whatever they had on special. Cod and red potatoes, it turned out. DiMaio, who owns the place and pours drinks for fun, came by and said hi. He used to be a studio guitarist, and worked with some pretty big heavy-metal names back in the day. But he got out of it because of the drugs, and now all that's just memories on his wall.

"Hey, Rick-o." He clapped my shoulder while I had a fork in my mouth, and it clanked up against one of my crowns. He had a fresh dye job on his hair—he still kept it long and jet black like in the glory days, so he looked like he did in all those pictures he never shut up about. "Have a beer?"

"Not tonight, thanks." I didn't like to drink before sex with Bev, which I guess wasn't much different from her not wanting to eat. DiMaio winked at me like he knew all about it, and left me alone. Right then I would've killed to have a brew with somebody I really loved, though. Some sweet girl, twenty-five or twenty-six, who just wanted to kick back and watch me teach our babies how to play baseball or hammer nails. Somebody who'd already done all her running around, and decided it was time to stop and cut her losses.

But that was some other Rick Bedrosian. The real Rick headed for the beach once the tide went out and saw Bev coming down the hill from her house, carrying a blanket and wearing one of her husband's sweaters. I was wearing one too, a tan V-neck, and had a couple more in a trunk at the shop.

"Excuse me, miss." I tried to sound like a cop, but it didn't work. "Can I help you find your way back to your house?"

"You don't need to know about my house," Bev said back. And she really meant that, because she never invited me over even once. The closest I ever got was her kitchen window, where I sneaked up one night after we beached it. All I saw was her flossing her teeth in front of the TV. "I'm the same in there as I am out here."

"I'm sure you are." I put my hand on her belly and gave her a little lick on the ear. She giggled and took my hands in hers, and we stood there face to face in the middle of the road. She had to be ovulating, I figured, or she wouldn't be acting all soft and fuzzy—not that it mattered with her tubes tied. She kept hold of my hand like we were sixteen, and we walked to the edge of the rocks and stood there watching a sliver of moonlight flicker on the waves.

"Makes me wish I played the guitar," I told her, because she wasn't saying anything. It made me jumpy just to stand there and not hear her talk, I don't know why.

"It reminds me of Portugal," she finally said.

"What about it?" I got goofy and kissed her hand.

"I was out on the beach, way south of Lisbon, and I fell asleep in the middle of the day. For maybe ten minutes, tops. But when I woke up there was this rose between my breasts, a yellow rose. And then this teenage kid, maybe sixteen, walking back and forth on the shoreline staring at me. I even waved to him once, but he didn't come over."

"How old were you?"

"Twenty-two, twenty-three. I was kind of a rich little brat."

"Did you think about fucking him?" I asked her.

"Wouldn't you? If a sixteen-year-old girl did that to you? Maybe not sixteen, but you know what I mean."

Then we started down the rocks to our little patch of sand, twenty feet square and fifteen feet down from where we stood. It was easy to get to once you knew the footholds, even in the dark. If you fell you might scrape yourself up pretty bad, but you wouldn't break anything because there was nothing but sand to hit. The place only existed at low tide, and that's why we liked it. If you looked down from those rocks at high tide, the waves would come up and whack you hard in the face, but with the tide low you could hang out on that patch of sand like the rest of the world didn't exist.

Bev got there first, and she had her hand on my belt the second my feet hit the ground. Our clothes started coming off, and we fell to the sand before the blanket went down. She always dragged that thing along and then forgot to use it. I let her push me onto my back, and the half-wet sand made cool little pinpricks against my skin. Above me the stars were coming out, and I looked for the Big Dipper while Bev started rubbing her nipples all over me — that was her big turn-on. I grabbed her by the hips a couple times and pulled her over me, trying to get inside her, but she'd always pull her legs together at the last second and make me try harder. Then she went back to rubbing at me till I got all worked up and went for her again. That was our big ritual.

On my fourth try she finally decided I wanted her enough, and let me in. We went right to it and humped around rough for a while, growling at each other and laughing and listening to the echoes in the little cave behind us, but then we settled down. Sometimes Bev would tell me a story or talk about her day once we started going slow, but I could never tell beforehand if she would. When she got real quiet and pulled her legs tight to my ribs, then I knew she was ready to come. She wasn't the kind who needed to come a million times — once was enough for her if she built up to it right and made me come with her.

"That old lady was funny today," she said. "Is that the one who wants to marry you off to her daughter?"

"Her daughter's friend." I leaned my head up, looking for Bev's breast, but settled for a little piece of skin on the inside of her arm. "Yeah, she's a hoot."

"I can't see you being married."

"Me neither. Not now, I mean, but I want to try it someday."

"Good luck." She ran a nipple in front of my mouth, but I just missed it. "Don't marry a banker."

Then she hummed a little and her hips found a groove, and we drifted off into our own thoughts. I wondered who I'd pick if God put a gun to my head and told me I had thirty seconds to choose a wife. A few girls passed through my head, but nobody I'd ever slept with. The only one who stuck out was this twenty-year-old from Texas named Bonnie, who I met when she was working at a coffee shop in Fort Lauderdale and hadn't thought about in years. She had these forgiving eyes that made me think I'd be happy forever if I married her, and I didn't just feel that way in hindsight either. I felt it right then. Those eyes looked like they could let an awful lot of my bad behavior slide, if I'd just let hers slide too. If you can forgive each other like that, then there's no use doing anything you'd need to forgive each other for — you just love each other as hard as you can, and that's that. I remember kicking myself for walking out of that coffee shop and leaving town without at least telling her I could love her forever, but it never would've done much good anyway. I was twenty-seven and wild then, with a big beard and eyes like arson.

Bev must've been thinking about somebody special too, because she leaned down and gave me her breast and things got really slow. I made believe I was in her bedroom, that when we got done making love we'd fall asleep and I'd feel her hand twitching in mine while she dreamed. At least if I got inside her house I'd have a little better idea what it was like to be married, to have your stuff all tangled up with somebody else's. And then once I knew what it was like, Bev could teach me how to let that fantasy go for good, so I'd stop wanting to try it out. So I could save myself the trouble.

"Tell me about Portugal," I said when Bev sat up and leaned back, straightening her spine so she could breathe deep and come better.

"It's hot, all the buildings are white." She lifted her knees and squeezed my ribs between her shins, almost ready to let go.

"No stories tonight?"

"No stories." She closed her eyes and belly danced side to side for a while, like I knocked her off her rhythm and she had to coax herself back to it. Above her head I saw what looked like a shooting star. I craned mine back as far as I could to follow it, trying to think up something between me and Bev that was big enough to wish for. Then I thought of Bonnie from Texas, or some girl like her I'd find if I hung around Rockport long enough.

Then when I couldn't crane my neck any farther I saw a face staring down at me, a towheaded kid who looked about thirteen and probably hadn't even hit puberty yet. His skin was shiny and white as blubber, and he stuck out like neon in the middle of the dark rocks and sky. His mouth dropped open and I felt mine do it too. Our eyes got wide and our hair stood on end and I came, just popped off inside Bev even though she wasn't ready for me yet. I let out a high-pitched little "Oh!," still looking up at the kid with my eyes as far back as they could go. My second "Oh!" was louder and scared him away. I saw a flash of elbow and bare chest and he was gone.

"That was a surprise," Bev said, rocking her hips fast and trying to get me going again right away.

"There was a kid up there." It was the stupidest thing I could've said. I should've just laughed and kissed her and asked if she could score me some Viagra.

"What?" Bev hopped off me faster than I've ever seen a woman move. She got to her feet, covered her breasts with the beach blanket, and crouched down to hide her ass in the cave. She looked up to the top of the rocks, but by then there was nobody left to see us. Bev grabbed whatever clothes she could reach and pulled them to her. "You're kidding me, right? What'd he look like?"

"I don't know, twelve, thirteen. Chubby face."

"Was he a redhead?"

"No, he was real blond. He looked kind of stupid, actually."

That seemed to calm Bev down. Maybe there was a smart, redheaded neighbor kid stalking her. Or maybe she had a redheaded son she never told me about, which would explain why she wouldn't let me near the house. She flicked the sand off her underwear and bra, and stood up just enough to put them back on.

"Don't lay there. I don't want people seeing you."

"They'll just think I'm skinny-dipping," I told her. I was on my side, not bothering anybody.

"I'm serious. Get me my shorts."

We got dressed and I started climbing back up the rocks, but Bev stopped me and said we had to take the long way around and walk through the water instead. I thought it was ridiculous. The kid was probably home in bed pawing himself by then, and I doubt he called the TV news crew on us. But I felt bad for him because he'd have me stuck in his brain forever. I'd probably look more and more like him every time he ran through that scene in instant replay, and one day he wouldn't be able to tell the difference between us. He'd feel me coming into Bev like it was his own real memory, and he'd wonder what happened to that kid who saw him. And who knew how long it would take him to want a woman any way but on top, with her long blond hair hanging down in his face. It's not like he'd be scarred for life or anything, but he'd turn into things he never would've turned into just because of what he saw me doing.

So with all that responsibility on my back, walking through a hundred feet of sharp rocks in rib-high water was the perfect punishment. Bev didn't say a thing, and the only time she touched me was when she lost her footing and grabbed my arm. We got back to dry land by the main beach, where there were a few tourists strolling around who could spy on us if they cared. None of them did. Bev stopped by the steps that led up to town.

"Okay," she said. "See you tomorrow."

"Yeah, sleep tight." I let her go up ahead of me so anybody who saw her would think she'd just decided to take a dip with her clothes on for the hell of it. She probably had a reputation in town for that sort of thing already. I waited a few minutes, watching the waves and wondering what kind of reputation I had. But there wasn't anybody in Rockport who'd known me long enough for that, so I went back to my shop and showered and went to bed. There was no heat on for the summer and the windows didn't do shit to keep the sea breeze out, so I put on two of Jeffrey Lillie's sweaters to keep from catching cold. Then I thought about that kid, that stupid fucking kid with his stupid mouth, over and over again till every kid I ever met looked exactly like him.

Bev never came around on Sunday like she said she would, so at sundown I went over to the rocks to look down at that patch of sand from the same angle as the kid did. The tide wasn't as far out as the night before, and the sand was covered with seaweed. I got on my stomach and leaned my head over the edge, like I was on the chopping block and somebody would come along any second to lop off my head. I tried to make the face I saw on that blond kid, the open mouth and the wide eyes and the hair standing on end, but there's no way you can force that kind of surprise. Maybe Bev coming up behind me would've done it. Bev grabbing me by the feet and trying to push me off the rocks so I'd never say anything about Saturday night to anybody.

But Bev didn't come, and when I had enough of staring at the sand I got up, brushed myself off, and went to Orry's to look for her. I got there and saw her with a pack of guys in the far corner, playing darts next to the jukebox. Bev's turn came up and she took the darts from Morrow, a skinny twerp who never shut his trap about real estate and the parties at Yale. He went to kiss her cheek when she stepped up to the line, and she didn't stop him. When she made her first throw, an electronic voice said, "Triple!" All the guys cheered.

I could tell Bev was wearing makeup, an orangey rose to go with her blue jeans and denim shirt and big turquoise earrings from New Mexico. She used to tell me she didn't believe in makeup, but I'm sure she wore plenty whenever she put herself on the market. She probably had it on the night I met her, too. There were eight guys playing darts with her—one of them a guy with a shop down the street from mine, who painted shitty seascapes on glass—all staring at her and waiting to see if she'd let them catch her this time. The new ones could already tell what kind of woman she was. And some of the old ones, like Morrow, must have waited years for their turn. I got sick of looking at all of them, and went to DiMaio at the bar to get a burger and a beer.

"Out of burgers, sorry." He looked up at the TV instead of at me. Women's golf. I'm sure he was a big fan.

"How about just a beer, then?"

"If you give Bev some space tonight. I talked to her, she wants you to lay off."

"I'll sit in a corner and she can come to me." I held my hands up, harmless. "I won't bother nobody."

"What if she doesn't want to come to you?" DiMaio leaned his hairy knuckles on the counter, looking pretty eager to get into a scrap with me. Maybe he wanted a chance to pull that big pipe out from behind his cash register and whack me in the head with it. Be the big hero, king of his own goddamn jungle.

"Tell her if she doesn't talk to me I'll burn her fucking house down." I put my fist on the bar right next to DiMaio's. Mine was huge compared to his, and hell if I was going to back down from a little runt like him unless he had that pipe swinging right at me. "Make it a pitcher, I'll sit back there and leave her alone."

"Better leave *everybody* alone."

I nodded and threw down twenty bucks while DiMaio drew me a cheap pitcher. I found the seat farthest from the jukebox, in the corner by the window where nobody likes to sit, and flipped through the fishing magazine I found there. Who really gave a crap about bigmouth bass and cutthroat trout? Just boring old guys in hip-high boots, freezing their asses off. They like the solitude, that's what they'll tell you. Being all alone in the woods, with nobody around to save them but themselves, though really they just want to get away from their wives. They spend half their lives working for one, then ditch her whenever they get the chance. Halfway through the pitcher I smelled hamburger coming toward me, and when I looked up I saw Bev carrying a plate.

"What's this about burning down my house?" She put the plate down, closer to herself than to me, and sat. Her face looked shiny as a cue ball from all that makeup.

"I'd never do that. I love your house." I pulled the plate my way and stuck some French fries in my mouth to stop myself from talking too much.

"You don't know anything about my house."

"I spied on you a bunch of times," I lied. "I've seen you yelling at your hubby on the phone."

That wasn't funny to Bev at all. "What do you want, Rick?" She pushed her chair out and leaned back in it, crossing her arms like I was going to throw a rock at her chest.

"Some kind of explanation would be nice."

"It's over. Things don't need a reason to be over."

"Was it me, or was it the kid?"

Bev rolled her eyes and looked away. I took a bite of my burger and stared at her while I chewed. I guess I could've called her a whore and she could've called me a whore and we'd scream at each other all night, and DiMaio would come out with the pipe and we'd make the papers. But it would never add up to anything more than it already was. I'd still hate myself for screwing people like her, and I'd keep pretending I wasn't one of them too.

"You make me feel like a whore," I said after I swallowed.

"You can feel like whatever you want to, Rick. I can't tell you what to feel like." She got up and kissed her fingers, then brushed them against my lips. "Say goodbye. It was good, but it's gone."

I didn't say goodbye. After I finished supper I went back to the shop and pulled some boards out of my van, set them on the lip of the bumper, and rolled my forge inside. I crated up my propane tank and bolted it to the wheel well, folded up my tables and my BACK TOMORROW! sign. The old guy who lived above the ice-cream shop across the street came out to his balcony and flicked on the light.

"Everything okay?" he said. His face glowed pink from the neon sign underneath him. There was nobody else around, only him and me. Not the last memory I wanted to have of Rockport.

"Yeah, it's just me. Just cleaning up."

He recognized my voice and went back inside. I loaded up my tongs, my anvil, my trunk and suitcases. Apron, gloves, box full of money. The last time I packed up to move I counted seventy-two things, and this time I had sixty-eight. Coffeemaker, blender, frying pan, boom box. I was getting there, I told myself. Fifteen or sixteen more moves, and I'd have nothing left but me. The only thing that takes any time is deflating my air mattress, which takes forever. But that was good, because it gave me a chance to fold up the nice sweaters Bev lent me and write out a note. All I could say was FOR MR. JEFFREY LILLIE, so I left it at that. Big letters on legal pad that I went over twice with a fat black marker.

At about eleven-thirty I rolled down the hill and stopped at Orry's again. It was practically empty, no surprise for a Sunday night. New Englanders still have enough religion left in them to go home early on a church day, or at least enough guilt left in them. There was heavy metal on the jukebox, with DiMaio singing along in falsetto while he dried off a beer mug behind the bar. Before I got there Morrow came out of the bathroom, stumbling drunk, and poked his finger into the middle of my chest. At least it wasn't him Bev left with.

"*Peter Peter, Pumpkin Eater,*" he sang right in my face. I grabbed him by the wrist and twisted. "Hey, that hurts."

"Cool it, Rick," DiMaio called. He puffed out his chest and crossed his arms over it. I pushed Morrow toward the door and went up to DiMaio.

"I'm not serving you," he said, and watched Morrow go out.

"I'm not asking you to."

"Then what do you want?" He put his hand by the cash register, waiting for me to make a move so he could grab the pipe. "You want a fight, there's always bikers down at Mako's."

"I don't want a fight."

"So spit it out. I'm busy."

"I just want to know if you fuck her when there's nobody else around to fuck her. That's all."

"That's a stupid-ass question." DiMaio laughed to himself, took another mug from the sink, and started drying it. His hand was nowhere near the pipe, so I guess the scare was over. "Tell me what you want to hear, Rick, and I'll say it to you."

"No, that's all right. I just wanted to ask it."

"Okay." He waved the beer mug at me. "You have a nice life now."

I saluted him and went back to my van, hoping Morrow would be out there singing, *Had a wife and couldn't keep her,* so I'd have an excuse to break his skull. But since there was nobody creep-

ing around in the shadows, I fired up the V-8 and headed south
for Gloucester. I knew I could find a bar there to zombie out
at, a place to crash in the van for the night, another girl to feed
me and fuck me awhile. But that was the same old crap I always
pulled whenever life sucked, and I thought maybe it was time to
do something different. Time to change everything—become a
monk, grow stuff out of the ground, marry that bridesmaid like
Mrs. K wanted me to, raise llamas. Be an investment banker or
play heavy-metal guitar and open up my own bar, be everybody's
friend till somebody stepped across the line.

Once the lights of downtown Rockport were behind me I
could breathe easier and stop thinking my life was so bad just because of what happened with Bev. It wasn't a total mess—I was
a free man, more than I can say for most. Maybe I didn't have
to change absolutely everything about my life, after all. But I'd
change whatever I could, and if I couldn't find a way to change it,
then I guess it was really me. And I could live with me, like I always have, even if it means running away from stuff the second
things get bad. If you don't have your own place to crawl back to
and your own people to stick up for you, then running is a hell of
a lot smarter than hanging around to fight for something that can
never be yours anyway.

The road out of Rockport curves close to the ocean, and sometimes you have to watch out for people running across it, going
back and forth from the beach to their cars. But I knew I wouldn't
see anybody running on my way out of town, not that late on a
Sunday night. I let my mind go for a bit, thinking about Portugal and Bonnie and how Jacob was doing with his girl in South
Carolina, and then I swear I saw that blond kid from the night
before in the middle of the road, wearing bright red swim trunks
and carrying a beach ball half as big as he was. It scared the shit
out of me, and I jammed on the brakes before I was anywhere
near him. He went away for a second, but when I hit the gas he
was there again, looking younger than he did on the rocks. His
mouth hung open just like it did when I was coming into Bev,
like that's the way he always looked and there was nothing special

about the face he made watching me. Maybe there wasn't. Maybe
he'd been following Bev around since before I came along, and
had her timed out so he knew when she'd be down on the sand
with somebody. Probably watched us fucking half a dozen times
before the night I caught him staring.

But he had to be in my head. How could it really be him, at
almost midnight on a Sunday and five miles away from home?
Just standing there, bouncing his ball on the asphalt and not even
looking up at my lights? He didn't run for the shoulder and didn't
look stuck or scared. He just stood there staring past me even
though I honked and honked, and there's no way a real person
does that. Not even somebody on drugs. Then he looked older,
maybe sixteen and filled out with his hair all spiky, so I knew I
had to be making him up. I blinked and he was gone, so when he
came back I didn't stop for him. I slowed down though, and heard
a thunk underneath me when I went by. It wasn't loud enough to
be a person, but I had to see what it was. And if it really was him,
if I really couldn't tell the difference between shit I made up and
shit that was right in front of me — then God love you, Rick.

I stopped on the shoulder, honked a few times, and cut the engine. Then I grabbed my flashlight and started looking around,
practicing saying "I'm sorry" for when I found him on the road
with his legs crushed. But the noise turned out to be just a hub-
cap that got crushed so many times it looked as thin as a dime.
No kid anywhere. I looked on both shoulders, but there was nobody.

"Do you need help?" I yelled out a bunch, crawling around on
my hands and knees, and every time I held my breath waiting for
somebody to answer. I even ran my fingers over the asphalt where
I thought I hit him to check for blood, too.

There was nothing. I got in the van and the kid showed up
again a couple miles later, but this time I drove straight through
him without slowing down. And the next time, and the next time,
till I finally made it to Gloucester. Drove right through him and
didn't hear a sound.

Me and Paul

I STILL THINK it was the woman who made me a liar, who made me want to be something I wasn't. Because in regular life I never lie to get something I want for myself, only when I need to keep my friends from bottoming out. When they aren't sure who they are anymore and need somebody to say "Hey, you're doing great, you're hanging in there," or tell them they didn't just mess things up forever with the person they loved the most in the world. Growing up, I was taught that a lie like that is the same thing as kindness, and it's a lot cheaper too, most of the time. You say the nice thing and you're done, you move on, and you keep away from the person you lied to for a while so you don't have to think up another lie to tell them later.

But in the middle of September I hooked myself on a lie that might've been the nice kind, and might've been another. I'd been hiking and camping up in Yellowstone to clear my head, walking the ridges and looking down at the tourists jamming up traffic for every moose, elk, or buffalo that came anywhere near the road. I got sick of it two days before I thought I would and checked my atlas to see if there was anything else to do in Wyoming before I headed back to Denver. Jackson? Too full of rich people, who needs it. Riverton and Lander? No idea what they

were about—probably nothing. The little red print next to Thermopolis said WORLD'S LARGEST MINERAL HOT SPRING, so I
pointed my truck there and showed up at eight Thursday night.
I followed the signs through town and found the TeePee pools,
which were still open for another couple hours. I paid for my
ticket, hustled into the locker room to change so I'd get my money's worth of time, and didn't bother showering like I was supposed to before I got into the water. Big sin, I know.

Now I'm a hot springs person in general, and it's hard for
me not to like one, but you can't class Thermopolis with Glen-
wood Springs or Steamboat Springs back in Colorado, the places
I end up going most. Thermopolis has a shitload of water, sure
—WORLD'S LARGEST—but there's only a couple pools hot
enough to really matter. Most of them are like bathwater after
you're done with your bath. And it's hard to really relax because
there's too many screaming kids playing volleyball or basketball or going down the waterslides. Usually at a hot spring I can
find a quiet spot and some water hot enough to boil me back to
my senses, but not at Thermopolis. To be honest, I couldn't even
feel the heat with all that screaming around me. I'm not saying I
hate kids, just that I'm not real good at filtering things out. Noise
goes straight to this one little nerve in the middle of my brain
that tightens up my skin, and my whole body turns into one giant
eardrum.

Anyway I got over it, like I always do. I spent most of my time
in the hottest pool and cooled off in the lukewarm one by the wa-
terslide, where I saw a blonde shooting baskets with a nine- or ten-
year-old kid who had to be her son. Right away I could tell there
wasn't a husband—I knew it from the way she held that ball up
over her head and made him jump for it. Higher and higher till
she decided he earned it, pushing him the way she thought a man
would. They had a game going that I couldn't understand, taking
three long-distance shots at a time and chasing down each other's
rebounds. I floated around, drifting toward them, and waited for
the ball to come my way.

The woman came from farm people, I could tell that just from looking at her arms and shoulders. Pale white skin, but with a little gold underneath—not the kind of pasty white that gets flabby. Her fake-blond hair came down to her chin, and she had that thin, sharp nose I always fall for. She was a regular person like me, not flashy or stupid or stuck inside herself. I'd never dated a woman with a kid before, or even asked one out, and maybe that's why I ended up lying. I had to be somebody new to do something new, I guess.

Well she and her son couldn't sink a basket to save their lives, and it was just a matter of time before that ball got into my hands. They chased it down again and again and the mom cheered every time her son managed to even hit the rim. He never cheered when she hit the rim, and I thought that was snotty of him, but since he didn't have a dad I couldn't get on his case too much. Right after I thought that, the ball came out to me.

"Whoa!" I said to the kid, careful not to look at his mom yet. "You're putting too much arm into it. Shoot from your toes, not from your shoulders."

The son looked down, like boys do if they aren't used to men telling them they're wrong. When a kid has a dad, he knows he's going to be wrong sometimes, and he knows his dad's going to tell him so. Without a dad, it's a slap in the face whenever a grown man says you're wrong. I bounced the ball against the water like an NBA pro at the foul line, then swished it through even though I hadn't shot a basketball in three or four years.

"Nice shot," the mom said, and she swam toward the basket to fetch the ball for me. Her eyes turned out to be a bright flashy green, and she had a nice little gap in her teeth. My dad told me gap teeth were sexy when I was a little kid, and I believed him. Still do. They made the whole rest of her face come together, and right before the lie started churning in my head I thought I could spend the rest of my life with those teeth. The blonde looked at my chest and arms, then tossed the ball back. She didn't have a ring on.

"Thanks," I said. "What's your son's name?" I threw the ball to him a lot harder than he was used to from his mom, but he caught it fine.

"Jay. Say hello to the man, Jay."

"Hi," the kid said without any tone to his voice. He went back to shooting the ball just like before, pushing it straight out with his arms and missing.

"Ask the man his name, Jay."

"What's your name?" the poor kid asked without even looking at me. It made me want to be his daddy for a day, just long enough to wipe that sad, going-nowhere look off his face.

"Paul," I told him. "Paul Chalmers. Your mom's pretty good at teaching you basketball, huh?" I looked at her and she laughed, shaking her head.

"I'm Tracy," she said, and waved. I never got a last name. "Where you from?"

"Down in Denver. I was up in Jackson awhile, looking at some old cars."

"Old cars, huh?" She sounded like she knew something about them, or at least liked them. When Jay missed again the ball bounced out to her and she jumped up to grab it over her head. She shot on the way back down and missed.

"I've got a vintage car dealership down in Cherry Creek," I said. "You know Denver at all?" The ball came to me, and I hit that shot too. I rushed in and scooped up the ball and tossed it to Jay, who finally shot it from his toes like I told him. Swish. I high-fived him, then passed the ball out to his mom.

"Been there once," Tracy told me. "Went to a Broncos game when I was twelve."

"It hasn't changed much in ten years." That got her laughing, because we both knew she was way past twenty-two. She missed another shot and I made a fancy one, a diving hook. I was never so good at basketball in my life.

"How about fifteen years?" Tracy put her hands on her hips and looked at me sassy. "How about seventeen?" Then she half-splashed some water at me, and by then I knew she didn't have too many chances to flirt in a town like Thermopolis. Especially with guys who'd talk to her kid, which I hear matters a lot to single moms. The ball came to me again and I started to shoot, but I knew I'd miss—don't ask me how—so I tossed it to Jay instead.

"Start with your feet," I told him. "It's like a spring, it goes all the way from your toes to your fingertips." He shot the ball and missed and I threw it back, saying "Keep trying." He hit two out of every five, and even made three in a row once.

"You lived in Denver all your life?" Tracy asked me.

"I was born in New York, but I was two when we moved. You're from here?"

"Oh yeah, born and bred. My dad was a lawyer, which is kinda crazy 'cause you wouldn't think we'd need a lot of lawyers up here."

"That's true, I wouldn't."

"He worked on the reservation, mostly. Sort of a do-gooder."

"You sound mad about that."

"Not really. It's just every girl here wishes she grew up someplace more exciting."

"Like Denver?"

"Hell, even Cheyenne. Even Sheridan! Wouldn't you like that, Jay?" He came out toward her after fetching a wild rebound, and she put her hand on his shoulder.

"Chicago!" Jay shouted, shaking off her hand. He jumped up and down, banging the ball on the water and splashing all of us. "Chicago! Chicago! Chicago!"

"His daddy's folks are there," Tracy told me. "That's where he wants to go."

"What's his daddy do?"

"Oh there's no daddy anymore." She held her ring hand up, empty. "Isn't that right, Jay?"

But Jay didn't answer. He was still bouncing and banging the ball down hard, yelling "Chi-CA-go, Chi-CA-go, Chi-CA-go!" He sounded like the little engine that could, trying to get himself up the hill of life without a daddy. *I know what that's like,* I wanted to tell him. *I know how to help you through.*

"Why don't you go find Floyd," Tracy told Jay in a firmer voice than I thought she had in her. But the kid was off in his own world, banging the ball and chanting "Chi-CA-go!" some more, and it took her a while to get his attention. "Don't make me start taking stuff away from you. Don't make me tell Mr. Grant I do your homework for you."

That was hard to listen to, and playing Jay's daddy for a day didn't sound so hot anymore. He started whining and crying and banging the ball in the water, splashing his mom's face. Tracy grabbed Jay by the ear, dragged him over to the other side of the pool, and finally said the right thing to stop his tantrum. He got quiet as a snail, climbed out, and walked over to the locker room with his head hanging so low I could barely see it over his shoulders. I didn't want to know what she said to him. Tracy turned back to me, smiling and tucking a strand of hair behind her ear. Then she waved at me like a teenager, stretched her arms above her head, and dove in. She aimed herself wrong and swam straight past me underwater.

"I hate doing that, Paul," Tracy said when she found me again. "His uncle Floyd works here. Probably sold you your ticket."

"I remember him. Mustache, right?" It was a wild guess, because I was pretty sure a woman sold me my ticket.

"Yeah, that's Floyd. He straightens Jay out whenever I can't. You have kids?"

"Nope." I held up my ring hand, as empty as hers. "How long has Jay gone without a daddy?"

"He was three when Jeff died. So two-thirds of his life, like he says. When he's sixteen he'll be telling me he's lived thirteen-sixteenths of his life without a daddy."

"He won't be saying that, not at sixteen. He'll be off finding his own daddies, or pretending he never needed one."

"This from experience?"

"Mine died when I was eleven. He had a Ford dealership with another guy and it went bad, and he shot himself in the head."

"Oh, that's terrible." She covered her mouth for a second. "You didn't find him dead or anything, did you?"

"No. He did it in the mountains, as far away from us as he could get."

"Wow." Tracy did a little backstroke all the way around me, I have no idea why. "So I guess that explains a lot. You dealing cars, I mean."

"Absolutely. Had to finish what Dad started."

"You got people working for you?"

"Three salesmen, a couple mechanics, an office manager. Plus there's a few guys out on commission. And a woman too, down in Santa Fe."

"What's your favorite car?" For the first time Tracy got close enough to touch me, but she didn't. "Or is that too hard a question?"

"No, it's easy. A nineteen sixty-five Buick Wildcat convertible. Looks kind of like an old Cadillac, but a little meaner. I fell in love with it when I was six and it took me twenty-five years to get my first one."

"How many do you have now?"

"Three," I said. "Plus the one up in Jackson I might buy."

"I wouldn't mind seeing that one, if you need a second opinion." This time Tracy did touch me. She rested her palm on my forearm before she pulled it away, laughing, and dove underwater again.

Every couple nights since I went to Thermopolis I stay up late and try to count all the lies I told Tracy. I get up to a certain number — seventeen usually, or twenty-two — then start sweating hard. I feel my pulse in my thumbs, feel a knocking in my left arm that makes me scared I'm going to have a heart attack. Then I imagine Tracy next to me in bed after sleeping with me for a week or a month or a season, crying her brains out on the day she finds out I've been lying to her all along. Her head's on my shoulder and she's digging her fingernails into my skin till I bleed.

"You didn't have to lie," she tells me. "I would've loved you. I would've moved to Denver for you, would've married you."

Then right in front of my eyes she turns into a different Tracy.

Not the too-cute-for-her-age blonde I met in Thermopolis, not
the one who still had hope. But somebody who lost that hope all
at once, who got old overnight and stopped taking care of herself. Somebody who didn't even like her own son anymore, who
turned into a hag just to get him out of her life so she could be
miserable alone. So she could drink vodka in front of the TV
watching game shows, or pop the pills her nurse friends sold her.

And I was the guy who made Tracy lose her hope. She believed
in me when she met me, and for a little while she put the whole
weight of her life onto me, but I turned out to be just a lie. Once
she found out I wasn't who I said I was, she couldn't trust herself
to tell the difference between a real person and a liar anymore. So
there she was in my bed, crying on my shoulder. Hollow inside,
because I made her feel that way.

But none of it ever happened. Tracy was never in my bed, and
I never saw her other than that one time in Thermopolis. Never
told her that my real name is Joseph Allan Ducek, or that my father never owned a Ford dealership or shot himself in the head.
Last year he retired after forty years as a maintenance man for the
city of Denver — his first job, his only job. He plowed snow, ran
street sweepers, bulldozed, fork-lifted. Anything you could drive
to clean stuff up or move it from one place to another, my father
drove. My mother is a substitute elementary school teacher who
can bake any dessert in the world. I have a younger brother I see
almost every weekend and only fight with for fun. It's a happy
family and I love it, and there was no reason in the world for
me to lie to Tracy when the truth would've been so much better.
When the truth could've gotten me a wife, maybe, and a stepson
too. But there's nothing I can do about it now except stay up and
count the lies I told her. Seventeen. Twenty-two. I got up to thirty
one time.

I've only seen a 1965 Buick Wildcat convertible once in my life,
when I was nineteen. I don't own a vintage car dealership and can
barely tell the difference between an Audi and a Maserati. I make
my living as a foreman for a company that manufactures large

molded fiberglass pieces—swimming pools, septic tanks, things like that. On the job I wear so much covering to keep out the stray fiberglass that you can't even see my face. I don't own a house in Cherry Creek, which is one of the richest parts of Denver, but rent an eight-hundred–square-foot apartment in Thornton, which is a strip mall suburb on the interstate. I'm thirty-two, though Paul Chalmers told Tracy he was thirty-seven. I had two years of college at a state school in Grand Junction, but Paul Chalmers had an MBA from Cornell.

On the nights I'm not beating myself up over how I lied to Tracy, I'm making believe I really am the things I told her I was. That my house has eight bedrooms and I can drink champagne whenever I feel like it. That I've got a bottle handy all the time, sitting in a silver ice bucket outside my bedroom. I fantasize about Tracy forgiving me for all the lies I told her, maybe even helping me turn into the person I said I was. But I can never forgive myself for those lies, not even when I'm making believe they're true. Not even when I close my eyes and turn into everything I said Paul Chalmers was, and have all the money I could ever need.

Anyway me and Tracy stayed in the big pool, talking about everything from my camping trip in Yellowstone to her high school friend who turned into a TV actress. From the scare I had with the IRS a couple years back, because of some workers' comp mistake, to her son's problems in history class. The longer we talked the softer Tracy's eyes got, the rounder her cheekbones got, and the more time her cleavage spent above the waterline. We took the slide down together even though we weren't supposed to, and her arms and legs felt great tangled up with mine. We were practically the last people in the place, and Floyd finally came out to yell through his hands that they were closing in fifteen minutes. We talked some more and Floyd said they were closing in five. Then he came back again and said they were closed.

Tracy didn't move once, except to wave at him the first time he came out. Ten minutes after closing, Floyd poked his head through the door and shouted, "Going home in five!" Then he turned and let the door slam, and I got a bad feeling that Tracy was lying to me just as much as I lied to her. Maybe not lying, really, just forgetting to tell me that I wasn't the first out-of-town guy who played basketball with her son and ended up watching Floyd shut down the TeePee pools. I could've been number three, or seven, or sixteen.

But I didn't ask her about that, because it didn't matter. Once you're past a certain age and a certain point of desperation, the only debate you have about whether or not you'll sleep with the person in front of you happens inside your own head—they've got almost nothing to do with it. You know how to get them in the sack if you need to, how to get yourself in the sack. You know how to surrender, how to make somebody else surrender. After Floyd's last pop-in, me and Tracy went to the locker rooms and met outside by the front door. Then I walked her over to her truck.

"It's been fun," I said, pretending to wrap things up even though we both knew we'd go to her house. "I had a great time."

"Then let's go do something. It's Jay's night for a sleepover with his uncle." She looked through the window and saw Floyd scowling in the lobby. "Be right back."

She went over to kiss Jay goodnight, but he was crying so hard she had to grab his head to do it. Floyd pointed at me and had some sharp words for Tracy, but I turned my head around and looked at the sky, listened to the wind in the trees. I thought up some problem back at my dealership that I could tell Tracy about if I had to—the guys in the garage not getting along—and before I knew it she was back next to me, tugging my arm. Floyd locked the front door of the TeePee behind us.

"Hey," Tracy said with her shoulder half against mine. "Jay always hates sleepover nights. Most of the time I go out with the girls, but they're all busy with their husbands tonight."

"Where do you and the girls go?" I leaned my shoulder into hers a little.

"Each other's houses, mostly. But that red motel on the highway's got a nice bar."

"Let's go there, I'll take you out." My face got a big, wide smile, like I was ready to spend more money on her than anybody in her whole life.

"Okay, but I have to stop home first. You mind swinging by?"

I followed her in my truck, knowing we'd never get to that bar and trying to figure out how she'd get me into her house. Wondering if she'd notice how rusty and old my truck was, and make me add to my lie by telling her I only used it for backwoods driving. The whole trip over I wondered if I'd have to go back to being Joe Ducek anytime soon, or if I'd get stuck so deep in being Paul Chalmers that I'd never crawl out of him again. Wondered if I'd get back to Denver and drive straight to my dealership, letting my truck show me the way.

It took about five minutes to get to Tracy's house, which was on the way east out of town. Actually in East Thermopolis, I found out later on when I looked at a map. Her road snaked off to the left a couple miles past the highway and turned to washboard. Then it turned to asphalt again and finally concrete, and we stopped at a white house that looked like a trailer with some extra rooms tacked on. I idled next to her and she left her engine running while she hopped up the steps and went in — to change her clothes, clean the place up, put in a diaphragm, whatever. Five minutes later she came back out again with the same clothes on, and she didn't look at me as she walked down the steps to her truck. I figured she was sending me away, sending me back to being plain old Joe D. She leaned in to cut her engine and I watched her taillights go out. Then she came over to me.

"I'm sorry," Tracy said, her face looking puffy like she'd been crying. "All I really want is somebody to hold me. I'm sorry to be pathetic about it, but that's what I need. I don't want to go out for a drink."

"Nobody says you have to." Women who don't drink tend to keep their clothes on, so I figured I was in for a night of listening to her talk. But I could handle it — Paul Chalmers could handle it, at least. "It's not pathetic at all. I'm glad you told me straight out."

"Nice of you to say that." Tracy didn't look up.

"There's nobody else to hold you?" Her fingers were on the little bit of window that stuck up from my door, and I put my hand on them.

"It's a little town. Everybody's taken, unless you want to cheat. And I don't."

"Mmm." I closed my eyes and ran my fingertips across her knuckles. Tracy moved her hand fast and grabbed three of my fingers. To this day I can't remember which three they were—they change in my mind all the time. "Don't cry," I told her, then got out of my truck.

"I'm not crying. I'm not even close to crying."

But she was, and did for the whole walk up to her door. If she kept crying after that, I would've had to get out of there or start crying myself. She held my hand for a second, dropped it, then let it thunk against hers while we walked. When she opened the front door and turned on the lights I saw the place was a trailer with some extra rooms tacked on, just like it looked from outside.

"Here's home," Tracy said.

"Nice job." I wasn't lying, because the place looked anything but trailer-trashy. Neat and organized, a couch with throw pillows on it, nice bookshelves, family pictures on the wall above the TV. Not a lot different from the house I grew up in, but of course I couldn't tell Tracy that. Paul Chalmers grew up with an alarm system and a stereo that piped into every room of the house. But Joe Ducek could put his mom and dad and brother at Tracy's kitchen table, and they'd fit right in. They'd even know where she kept the tin foil and the ketchup.

"Did your husband put all this together?" I asked. I figured she'd like me asking about Jay's dad—she probably still loved him, probably asked him to forgive her every time she slept with another guy.

"No, Floyd did. He's my lifesaver. After Jeff died, I couldn't keep the old house."

"Does your brother like taking care of Jay?"

"Let's not talk about that." Tracy started for the kitchen but stopped and turned back, then walked straight over and wrapped her arms around me. Squeezed me and let me go, squeezed me and let me go—she did it four times and I stood there like a tree, letting her. I couldn't believe how soft she felt, how much she pulled me into her skin. Finally I squeezed her back—maybe not as hard as she did, or as hard as she wanted, but harder than any other rich guy from Denver ever would.

"I like being close to you," she said. "You're not pushing me away inside. Lots of people push me away inside."

"Why would they do that?" I stroked her hair and rocked her back and forth.

"They're scared of me. Like I've got a big sign around my neck that says NEEDY. Guys think I'll suck the life out of them, with a kid and all."

"I think you give more life than you take."

"That's sweet of you to say." Tracy broke the hug and pulled back to look in my eyes. Her hands went to my chest and I felt like I knew how things would go from there. Say nice things about each other for long enough to act like we're doing something more than fucking, then rip each other's clothes off. Screw like hell, lay down together, fall asleep like we're married. Wake up and say goodbye like we'd do it again that night, even though we didn't even get each other's phone numbers.

Not like I did that kind of thing all the time—once or twice at most, and I didn't want to make it a habit. Tracy got right to the point, yanking open a button on my shirt and biting me on the collarbone, and all of the sudden things went into overdrive. She kissed my throat and rubbed her hands up and down my belly fast, then pulled my hands to her breasts. I could barely touch them—it was happening too fast, and my hands just sat there.

"Don't you want them?" she asked me.

"I do. But kiss me first." We started kissing, and I unbuttoned her blouse and tugged off her bra. Half a minute later she slid down her jeans, undid my buckle, and backed me onto the couch underneath her. It was weird—mechanical and fast, like I was stuck in a burning car and she was pulling me out. Then we slithered around on the couch and stripped each other down the rest of the way without talking. Tracy rubbed her hands on my cock, and her breasts too, but it wouldn't come up. It just laid there like a sponge, which isn't the kind of thing that ever happens to me.

Then I got worried—what if it happened to Paul Chalmers all the time? What if he tried getting it up with a bunch of women, going from hot spring to hot spring, and could never do it with any of them? Tracy sighed and sat back hard against the couch.

"You've got a wife," she said. "Don't you?"

"Yeah," I told her, looking away guilty. "I'm sorry I lied."

"I knew it." Tracy whacked herself in the forehead and laughed, but it was a miserable kind of laugh. She pulled a blanket from a chair, dark blue with gold swirls, and covered our crotches with it. "You're like men always are when they have wives."

"What do you mean?" I put my hand over her thigh and traced a swirl with my finger.

"Hot, then cold. At least you didn't go all the way and then spend the next year trying to weasel out of your marriage."

"Look, it's not you, I—"

"You don't have to say that, Paul. You did what you had to do." Her lips bunched together and the corners of her mouth turned down—I guess I wasn't worth her fake smile anymore. "You made another woman want you, and that's enough for you married guys."

"You got us figured out," I told her, and settled into the couch because I didn't feel like leaving yet.

"All I want to know is if you do this all the time. I mean, find a girl like me who's desperate, then quit once you get her where you want her."

"I'm not trying to. It just happens." I looked away and blushed so deep I couldn't have been anybody else in the world right then but Paul Chalmers—I was so far into being him that I had to lie my way out of him already. Paul was a guy with a wife in Denver and problems at home he couldn't solve. More problems than Tracy had, maybe. A guy who needed other women to touch him, but loved his wife so much he could never let those other women have him all the way.

"Look." Tracy put her arm on mine, done being pissed at me. "I said before I just want to be held, and I got that from you. Thanks."

"You're sure?"

"Yes, I'm sure. Now I've got to go pick up Jay."

I nodded and stood up, and Tracy turned her back to me while we put our clothes on. When I got done, I slid my hand into my pocket and pulled out my wallet. Tracy saw it and her face went three shades whiter than before. She waved her hand at me and backed away like the wallet was a gun.

"No, please. Don't do that."

"Take it." I pulled out the three twenties that were supposed to last me the rest of my trip. I still had five bucks left, plus a gas card that could get me home if it had to. "Please."

"I'm not a charity case, okay? Or a whore."

"I don't think you're a whore. How could I think you're a whore? We didn't do anything." I pointed at the couch like it was evidence.

"Men think what they want. If you give me money, in three days you'll think I was a whore."

"Take it," I told her. Paul Chalmers was used to people doing what he told them, period. "I've got plenty of it, you don't. Take it."

Tracy shook her head and still wouldn't take my money. I looked hard at her, really fixed her in my eye this time, then threw the money on her floor like I could afford to burn it. Tracy pretended to spit at the bills but didn't move otherwise, didn't even look at me, and when I went out her front door I slammed it as hard as I could.

I counted to five, then opened it back up and caught Tracy

reaching for the cash. She was so surprised she forgot to yell at me.

"What did you say to Jay in the pool?" I asked her. "Right before you sent him to Floyd. What did you say you'd take away from him?"

"His pictures of his daddy, okay? Now get out before I call my cop cousin."

I nodded at Tracy, closed the door, and stood on the front steps again. For a solid minute I thought about going back in—I never did hear her lock up. Thought about walking into her living room with a smile and telling her I wasn't Paul Chalmers at all, I was really Joe Ducek and didn't have a wife. Telling her I was a regular guy who could get it up, with a family just like hers. Telling her I was Joe Ducek and that I really liked her son, really wanted to hold her and love her and teach Jay how to do anything I could do.

But what if Joe Ducek turned out to be a lie, too? What if it wasn't just Paul? What then?

The Balkan House

THIS STORY ISN'T about the Iranian girl. She's maybe the reason I'm writing it, but she's not who it's about and not why things ended up like they did. This story is about a woman named Maura Danelow, who was going to take me to Virginia with her but instead left me stranded for nineteen days at a grimy little hole in Pompano Beach, Florida, called the Balkan House Motel.

I picked the place out myself because I knew what the name meant. In high school they taught me that the Balkans are a bunch of mountains over by what used to be Yugoslavia. They taught me that "Balkanize" meant "to break up into small, mutually hostile units." I remember all this because Yugoslavia was the big war of my high school years, and because we had a Serbian refugee family in town who everybody gave money to. They were Balkan, but they didn't look anything like the people who run the Balkan House Motel. Maybe the Serbs or Croats or whatever owned the place a long time ago, and named it after where they came from. But there's no reason to keep calling it the Balkan House anymore, because Iranians own it now — not rich Iranians full of oil money, like I used to assume they all were, but regular salt of the earth Iranians who have to work their asses off for everything they get.

I know that the family who owned it worked their asses off—or at least most of them did—because I saw them hustling all the time. Stocking the shelves in the little grocery store by the checkout desk. Hosing down the stairs and the concrete hallways even though they weren't that dirty. Scraping the doorframes and painting them blue, because the blue they already were wasn't quite bright enough. Going over the money at night in rooms 4, 5, and 6, shouting in a language their guests couldn't understand, one family Balkanized into three mutually hostile units with only the screen doors between them and the August night.

Somewhere there was a husband who I almost never saw, plus a wife who ran the show and spent most of her time in the grocery store. A grandma dressed in black who always stayed inside, a grandpa who putzed around and fixed little stuff here and there. A twenty-something son and his slightly lighter-skinned but still Iranian wife, who wore and drove fancier things than they could actually afford—they usually started the nighttime shouting matches. And of course there was the teenage daughter, who buzzed around doing all the errands grandpa told her to and who cleaned the rooms every morning.

At eleven sharp she'd knock on my door, and even after the first week I'd jump at the sound because I was always too busy daydreaming to expect it. I'd be sitting around reading the novels Maura gave me to kill the time, thinking how great life with her would be in Virginia, or why the hell I even decided to move up there, or what went wrong with my life that turned me into such a weathervane I could never tell a good wind from a bad one. Maura said I should go to the beach, which was only three blocks away, so I wouldn't be around when the girl came by. But I'm a northern person, with pale northern skin, and at that time of day I fry like a potato chip after five minutes of sun. I get my beach time at sunset, and would rather sweat like a hog in the shitty air conditioning of room 17 than burn to a crisp just to be out of the way when the girl showed up to clean my room. So I was there on August 18, just starting a new chapter of Stephen King's *Firestarter,* when the knock came.

"Time for clean sheets?" the daughter said. She had a slight accent, but the sing-song of her voice was like American teenage girls everywhere. Like kids who grew up watching TV and giggling together and roaming the school hallways in little packs. She'd probably spent more of her life in America than in Iran, but she wasn't born here—that much you could tell. She'd made herself maybe 85 percent American by then, and would probably work it up to 95 percent someday. But she'd never get the last 5 percent, and I liked that about her. It would've ruined her to be like everybody else.

"Just a minute!" I called, then stripped off my gym shorts and pulled on my bathing suit. I grabbed my straw hat and opened the door to go out. She stood in front of me, waiting next to her cart full of cleaning supplies and new towels and sheets. I don't know why she had so many sheets on the cart, because as far as I could tell there were only six people in the hotel other than her family. Maybe five, depending on what happened last night after all the fighting in room 12.

"Good morning," she said, sort of bobbing her head down. That must've been an old-country habit, one of those 5 percent things she maybe picked up from her grandparents.

"Morning," I said back, bobbing my head too. It was hard not to stare at her because she was one of those achingly beautiful teenage girls who's so pure and virginal that you want to build a temple around them. The kind of girl you look at with a little reverence—a feeling that's missing in the world today. She was thin as a snake and had unbelievable skin, this gleam of butterscotch and copper wrapped so tight around her muscles that she wouldn't even get wrinkles when she was eighty. She had delicate features except for her nose, which looked like an arrowhead and made me stare at her even more. Not because it was an ugly nose, since it wasn't, but because it looked so out of place on her. Like

God wanted to see what happened if he glued a forty-year-old man's nose onto this perfect, delicate, teenage face.

Anyway, I told her, "I'll be in the pool awhile," then grabbed my green beach towel from its hook by the door. I didn't really have to tell her where I was going because I'd done the same exact thing at eleven A.M. for eighteen days in a row by then. Go down to the pool and float there with my T-shirt on and my hat pulled over my face, say hi to grandpa while he putzed around cleaning. I could've gone to the pool at 10:55 every day and never run into the girl at all, but seeing her face in the morning gave my day more structure than Maura ever could. Maura and her phone calls that always made me jump, Maura and her "I'll be there in fifteen minutes" that always ended up stretching out to forty-five.

I slipped out while the girl was in the hall getting ready to push her cart in, then heard her humming some pop song that made me poke my head in the door after her. The second I heard her humming, she wasn't just the girl who cleaned my room anymore. She turned into somebody who liked things, who wanted things and didn't get them sometimes. Who thought about stuff she never told anybody else.

"What's your name?" I asked her. All I had sticking through the doorframe were my head and shoulders. No hands, nothing. I figured after eighteen days I ought to know the name of the girl who cleaned my room.

"Dalila," she said, ducking behind her cart so all I could see was her wiry black hair. I couldn't even see her hands — she had her yellow rubber gloves on already.

"Thanks, Dalila." I pronounced it her way. "Do they call you De-*ly*-lah at school?"

"Yes sir. The American way."

She turned and started pulling apart my bed. I felt her grandfather's eyes staring up at me from the pool, which took up half the motel's courtyard. When I waved at him he went back to scooping bugs off the surface and acted like he never saw me. I looked back to see if Dalila would smile goodbye, but she just stared at the floor. I wasn't trying to make her my best friend or anything, so I don't know what grandpa was so uptight about. But you get starved for human company when your girlfriend dumps you off without a car at a $29 a night motel, and anybody you see eighteen days in a row—at the same time of day, too—is practically a friend you can depend on. I headed down the stairs and nodded at the old man, put my hat on the edge of the pool, and dove in like I didn't even notice him scooping bugs. He frowned and said something in a language I didn't understand, probably swearing at me.

"I'll come back later," I told him, starting to climb out. "Sorry, my mistake."

"Is okay." Grandpa wiped his forehead and went back inside room 6. I knew he was sick of me, like everybody else at the Balkan House. Sick of the weird guy in room 17 who didn't like the sun, who never went anywhere for more than a couple hours at a time, who didn't even have his own car. Who came down every evening at six sharp to pay for another night's stay in cash, instead of paying by the week and saving himself forty bucks. Who sat around waiting for the gold car to come and park in space number 17, and never left that room when the gold car was there.

I don't think they ever figured me out. But then again I can't figure myself out either, so who can blame them?

Anyway I swam across the pool a few times, then slid a little foam board under my back so I could float with my arms spread wide. Once I got good and comfy I opened my eyes, and there was Dalila shaking out my bed sheet on the landing. This morning the sheet had a long pink stain in the middle of it, and she saw it as loud and clear as I did.

I should've kept my eyes to myself, because I knew where the pink stain on that sheet came from. The whiteness of it came from my semen and the redness came from the menstrual blood of Maura Danelow, who was the reason I'd been staying at the Balkan House Motel for eighteen nights in a row without knowing when I'd leave. Every day at five-thirty she'd call to tell me her divorce still wasn't final, how we had to wait till the next day again. Every day from five-thirty to six I'd think about leaving, think about asking Grandpa for a ride to the Greyhound station so I could buy a ticket out of town. Where? Back to Ohio? Fuck Ohio. So I'd go to the office at six and sign up for another night at the Balkan House, using the cash Maura slipped under my pillow.

When the sheet stopped fluttering on the landing, I saw Dalila's black eyes staring straight down at me — at the dirty American who didn't have a real wife, just a woman who came and went whenever she felt like and left pink stains on the bed. At the dirty American who didn't even know how long he wanted to stay. As I reached for my hat on the pool's edge to get the sun out of my face, I felt sure that Dalila was thinking exactly those thoughts. When I look back on it I always try to imagine some different kind of feeling in her eyes — a look that said she'd seen it all a hundred times and didn't care anymore, or a look of inner strength she got from knowing that she'd never sleep with a man before he married her. Knowing she'd always be right with herself and right with God — not like those dirty Americans, not like that guy with the bloody sheets in room 17.

The sheet went in the cart and my hat went over my face, and Dalila went back into the room to remake my bed. My phone rang — it had to be Maura, since nobody else in the world knew where I was — and I started out of the pool to answer it. But I didn't want Dalila hearing me talk to Maura, so I let it ring and listened to her working upstairs. Pushing her cart outside, running the vacuum cleaner for two or three minutes, then pushing her cart around the corner to room 23 where I couldn't see her anymore. But I could still picture her eyes — those half-judging, half-pitying eyes. That's the terrible thing about people with beautiful eyes, you can read any emotion in the world into them. Plus some that aren't in the world at all.

So I got stuck in Dalila's eyes awhile, instead of in Maura's like I had a right to. Stuck there until she finished room 23 and moved on to wherever she went next. I got out of the pool, toweled off, and went back to room 17. Then I crawled between the clean sheets Dalila put down for me, waiting for Maura to come over so we could get them dirty too.

Maura Danelow was my CPR instructor about eight months ago, when I decided I was finally going to get my act together and become an EMT like my best friend from high school. I passed that first class, but to be honest the rest of the EMT training was too much work for me. Too many books, too much to memorize, too much at stake if you fuck up. So I dropped the EMT program and kept on tending bar part-time, mostly under the table on weekends in Miami Beach and Coral Gables, and turned people on to my friend Mike the drug dealer for an occasional commission. Not all that noble, I'll admit. But all I took was phone numbers, never money, and other than a little bit of X I kept myself clean. You do things like that when you're a stranger in town, and after a couple months I knew that's all I'd ever be in Miami. Some people do a lot worse.

Well four months ago Maura and three of her girlfriends showed up in a bar where I was working happy hour, and they all flirted like hell with me. Maura knew where I'd be bartending because I mentioned it in class, so I guess she thought I'd give her free drinks or something. Which I did. She'd just filed for divorce, the girlfriends told me while she was in the bathroom, and this was the after-filing celebration. They'd all been her bridesmaids when she got married, and had all gone with her to the courthouse that afternoon as divorce witnesses. They planned to get plastered and take taxis home. They planned to chop Maura's husband up into little pieces and feed him to his neighbor's dogs. I asked them what he did wrong, and they all shook their heads and said I didn't want to know.

One of the bridesmaids flirted with me hard and got my number, then passed it on to Maura—a very slick move, I think, from a very good friend. Maura called me up two days later and told me how *genuine* I seemed to her that night in the bar. How *real* it felt to talk to a man who lived in his own true skin, instead of in a lie like so many do. A man who was strong in some ways and weak in others and could live with that, who didn't need to cover his weaknesses up with fake strengths that only rotted him out from inside.

"Are you asking me out?" I said when she caught her breath.

"No. But if you asked *me* out I'd say yes."

"Oh I see. One of those decisive women. You're not getting back with your husband, are you?"

"Fuck no. I'd rather be a nun than let him touch me again."

"Then ask me out, Maura. Don't be shy."

We went to Miami Beach that Friday night and made out in the sand. I asked about her husband but she didn't say much, and I figured she never would. Maura took me to a basketball game the next Tuesday, and on Wednesday we saw a movie and ate Cuban. At six A.M. Friday, when her shift at the hospital ended — she was an ER nurse — she came over to my apartment and fucked me without saying a single word. Then she cried. She slept over at my place for five nights straight, and by the next Saturday I felt like I could ask her about her husband again. I'd been dying to know ever since that night in the bar, when her friends warned me off asking.

"How would you feel if a man told you he sold dental equipment, and it turned out he was distributing kiddie porn?" She clamped her mouth shut, her lips as flat as possible. "You'd want to chop him into little bits, wouldn't you?"

After that, Maura spent half her time telling me about her husband's porn ring. I ended up knowing as much about the kiddie porn industry as I do about anything but bars and restaurants. It scared the shit out of me. Maura was only six months older than me, but back when I was taking her class it felt like ten years. Then, when I found out about her husband, I felt like a five-year-old. All this shit she'd lived through, and I could barely even tell people what I did for a living.

●   ●   ●

A no-fault divorce in Florida runs like this. After you file, you're considered legally separated for three months, and if you haven't patched things up by then you split your assets and debts fifty-fifty and go your merry way, provided you get a rubber stamp from the judge on your court date. Ten weeks into Maura's waiting period, after she'd sold most of her things and stashed the rest in my apartment, she got a job offer in Virginia Beach, Virginia, and asked me to move there with her. I thought about it for three seconds, decided yes, and then told her—just to pretend like she wasn't the only option in my life—that I had to sleep on it a few days. But after a year in Miami I had a whopping total of three guys I could call friends, and maybe ten who could get my name right half the time. I was this ghost who walked through the fringes of other people's lives without them even noticing me, and that's never a good thing. Maura asked me about the move three days later and I said I was leaning that way but still had to think it over, even though I'd been checking out Virginia Beach on the library computers and looking into jobs there. Maybe she could help me get a job at her hospital—lab tech or something like that. One of the guys who runs the empty stretchers up and down the halls. A regular job, with blue scrubs and a nametag.

So the next day I took her out for a nice dinner and said yes, I want to move to Virginia Beach with you—I didn't want her asking me a third time, didn't want her to feel like she was begging. We went back to my place to start packing stuff up and fantasize about how we'd lay out our new apartment, which the hospital would pay the first month's rent on. What kind of furniture we wanted, how big a TV to get, whether to jump up to a king-size bed or not. Maura did most of the talking, and it scared me how easily I could go along with everything she said. She could tell me she wanted to rob banks, and I'd say, "Sure." Tell me she wanted to open a scuba diving school in Cuba, and I'd say, "Sure." A vodka bar in China. Hey, why not?

I kicked myself about it at first, but then I realized I could just keep saying "Sure" to Maura and pretty soon I'd have a wife without having to bust my ass for one like most guys do. Save myself the heartache, save myself from getting turned down. And it's not like I didn't love Maura for real—I loved her plenty after just a couple months, and knew I could love her even more. I told her that often enough to keep her happy, which isn't easy with a woman who's getting divorced. I even said she could move into my apartment officially, and stop crashing on some girlfriend's couch every few nights just to pretend she wasn't living with me already. But she didn't go for it.

"We'd live together in Virginia Beach," I told her. "Why not now?"

"That's Virginia Beach, Jamie. Not Miami. Two different worlds."

Maura's divorce was finally due to come through August 7, after a month-long delay while her husband tried some plea-bargain with his porn lawyers. I moved out of my apartment on August 1 so we'd both be all packed up, and could drive to Virginia right after she left the courtroom—nice and symbolic. The only problem was, her husband kept on putting things off. One day he didn't show up. Another day he asked for an extension, telling the judge how he wanted to work things out with her. She told the judge that was a crock of shit, and she got fined for swearing in court.

By August 18 I'd been holed up in the Balkan House Motel for so long it felt like I was the one in jail, instead of the pervert husband. What the hell was I supposed to do, call my three friends and say, "Hi, it's Jamie I'm leaving town," and throw some big party they'd all be too busy for? Hang out at the diner down the street and try making friends before I left town? Maura got a lawyer to try forcing her husband's hand and spent a whole bunch of time on that, plus she took extra shifts at the hospital to cover for a friend. So all she ever had time for with me was sex and bitching about Roy, the hubby. Whenever she came over I told her I loved her, told her I'd wait for her forever if I had to. I took her money for the room and read all the books she gave me, almost one a day. I watched TV and masturbated thinking there might be some better woman in the world for me than Maura, but never let myself come. I was saving it all up for her, I told myself, because she needed it more than any other woman could. Needed a man to make her trust the world again, because it was a man who broke her trust in the first place. Even if that's all I did for her, even if I just got her to Virginia Beach and made her trust the world and then she dumped me there, I'd be fine with that. But I wanted to go soon, and I told her so every time she came over.

"Be patient," she'd tell me every time she left.

"I am patient. Look at me, I'm as patient as a fucking oak tree."

"Well stay patient one more day, baby."

Then she'd kiss me goodbye and I'd watch her gold car pull out of space number 17, sometimes with her waving from the window and sometimes not. Then I'd go back to reading or watching TV or jerking off, and wait for Maura to come back again. Sometimes she'd call to tell me she was coming, and sometimes she didn't. At noon on the eighteenth, after Dalila changed the sheets, I heard her engine. I looked through my window to watch her gold car zip over the speed bumps, then flopped down naked on the bed with the door propped open a crack. Maura came up, pulled off her nurse's scrubs, and jumped on top of me.

"He's such a bastard," she said, rubbing her hair against my stomach and kissing my chest. Then she started telling me all the miserable things Roy said and did that day.

"I don't want to hear about Roy," I told her. "Your life's not going to be about Roy for much longer."

"Who's it going to be about, then?"

"You and me." *Was that you, Jamie?* I wondered right after those words left my mouth. *Did you really say that?* I tried to keep Maura on top of me so maybe the sheets wouldn't get stained, so I'd never again have to see Dalila's eyes looking at me like they did that morning. But Maura liked to finish up with me on top, so that's how it went. When we got done we cuddled on the bed and of course the sheets were stained pink again. I looked at the spot, a little more oval than that morning's.

"You're really getting me out of here, right?" I asked her. "I'm losing my mind."

"Yes, we're absolutely getting you out of here."

"Even if you don't get him to sign?"

"I'll get him to sign," Maura promised. "He's just dragging things out to punish me."

"You're sure he won't keep doing it? Does he know I'm waiting for you?"

"I think so." She looked away.

"You *think so?* Anything more concrete than that?"

"I told him. Yes, he knows."

"You *told* him?" I sat up. "Fuck, hon. You're letting Roy jerk me around as bad as you. You're leaving me in limbo here."

"You're always in limbo, Jamie." She stood up, touched my chin real tender, and started putting her scrubs back on. "That's why I love you. You're so much better at limbo than me."

"Going back to work?" I said. I didn't ask her why it was fair to leave me in limbo just because I knew how to hang there better than she could.

"I'm covering Mona for half a shift. I'll come back and see you, though."

"Stay the night. It's no big secret if you told him about me already, is it?"

"I told him you existed." Maura looked at my pillow instead of my eyes. "I didn't say who you were, or where you were."

"Look, if he wanted to find us here, he would've found us already. Stay the night. You're torturing me."

"I *can't*," Maura snapped back. "It's bad for the trial. Plus you don't know what kind of people he hangs out with. This is child porn, Jamie. These aren't people you want knowing where you sleep."

For the next five hours I had imaginary conversations with Maura that I'd never have the balls to even start in real life. How bad she used me, how she didn't really love me, how I never got any closer to her than I was the first time we slept together. I growled a lot, saying all sorts of shit that sounded good coming out of my mouth as long as nobody heard it. But I'm glad I went through my angry phase, because by the time Maura got back to room 17 I didn't have any poison left in me. I'd washed the new pink stain off the bottom sheet, and it was still damp when Maura came back.

"That's silly," she said when I explained why I cleaned it. "The kid's family owns a motel. She's seen all sorts of stuff."

"But they're from Iran," I told her. "They shoot people for adultery in Iran."

"I don't think Iranians come to America because they believe in shooting people for adultery. They come because they *don't*."

"I guess so," I said, and it's all I felt like saying. Maura put her hand on my forehead to check my temperature, like moms do to their kids—it was the number one thing I couldn't stand about her, but she was a nurse and I had to learn to accept it. We'd had this conversation before. "Am I sick?"

"You're fine," she said, and right after that we made love again. Real slow and tender this time, and I wondered if that's the way married people do it after they have fights. If it is, then I can understand why people get married. You don't mind falling out of love every once in a while, because you know a nice, soft landing pad is waiting for you every time. Yeah, marriage was okay. I was about to say something profound about that when Maura asked me—

"What do you think about fish? Have you ever had a saltwater tank?"

"Lots of maintenance," I said. "If I'm working too, we won't have the time."

"You think you'll work?"

"Sure, I'll work." It pissed me off how lazy she thought I was.

"How about some easy-care fish then? Some goldfish."

"I'm down with goldfish," I told her. Then we slept until the air conditioning started to freeze us to the bone, and Maura got dressed again and left.

· · ·

At eleven on the morning of August 19, Dalila knocked on the door of room 17 again. I was already in my trunks and waiting this time—it only took me two and a half weeks to learn the drill—but after I opened up I stood in the doorway instead of heading for the pool like usual. I was going to talk to her, have a real conversation like you do with people you see every day. Not like she was my buddy or anything, but like we rode the same bus and chatted just to keep from being bored out of our minds. My sheets were clean—still wet from me scrubbing them down twice, but clean—and I didn't have anything to be ashamed of anymore. I wanted to see her eyes again, wanted to know they believed I could be more than just some guy who let a woman come over and dirty his sheets and leave.

"Time for clean sheets?" she said.

"They're fine," I said back. "But you can change them if you want to."

Dalila nodded and I stayed in the room while she pushed her cart inside. I took my time finding my sun hat because I wanted to see her eyes light up when she pulled the sheets off the bed and saw that they really were clean, like I told her. But she didn't start with the sheets that day, maybe because I was watching. She started in the bathroom.

"How long have you been in America, Dalila?" I asked her, saying the name how it's supposed to be said.

"Twelve years. Since I was three."

"You speak very good English."

"But my Farsi isn't so good." She half-laughed, but looked at the floor like people complained about her Farsi all the time.

"What do you want to be when you grow up?"

"A doctor." She squirted cleaner in the toilet and started swabbing it out.

"I used to want to be a doctor. The woman who comes to visit me, she's a nurse. Do you know who I'm talking about?"

There must've been something about how I said it, or about my body language, because right then Dalila stepped out of the bathroom and walked to the middle of the room. She didn't exactly run away from me, but she did give herself a lot more space to move in case she had to.

"Please, sir," Dalila said. "I can't clean the room if you're here."

"I'm not the kind of person you think," I told her, holding up my hands. "I need you to understand that."

She stood there a second with her eyes narrowed like she wanted to say something, like the thoughts were all lined up in her head but the words wouldn't spill out right. Then Dalila moved quick and sharp toward the door, and that's when I made my mistake. That's when I reached out to touch her arm and my hand got stuck on it somehow, caught in her elbow. She yanked away to get loose and ran out yelling for her family.

It was just supposed to be a little touch on her forearm with an open hand, tender and friendly like when you're about to tell somebody a secret, but it turned into a grab on the elbow. That little twist her upper body made when I touched her is what did it, what brought the whole gang up to yell at me in Farsi. Her grandpa spat at my feet and pushed me up against the wall. Five minutes later the cops showed up and handcuffed me for the first and only time in my life. I called Maura's cell with my one phone call from the police station, but she didn't check her messages until after sundown.

"You did *what?*" she yelled at me when she called back.

"My hand got stuck in her elbow, that's all. It sounds way worse than it was."

"Don't ask me for bail money, Jamie. I'm not marrying another creep." It was the first time she ever used that word on me, *marry.*

"Maura, it's not—"

"Forget it, okay. Fifteen years old, Jesus Christ!"

Then she hung up and we were finished. Two days later Dalila's parents dropped all the charges and brought my suitcases to the station. A cop explained the restraining order.

"Can I get a job with this on my record?" I asked him.

"Depends on what you call a job" is all he told me. So I went back to tending bar and working for Mike again, settling back into who I was before Maura. Into who I was supposed to be all along, I guess. You can take all the things I wanted to be when I was a kid—doctor, engineer, diesel truck mechanic, fishing guide—and all the things I tried to be, whether I wanted to or not, and all they add up to now is a guy who grabbed a fifteen-year-old girl by the elbow so he could tell her something he couldn't even say to the woman he loved. Couldn't say to the woman he was about to move away with, maybe for keeps.

What was I going to tell her? Who the hell knows. That moment's long gone.

Inside the Hole

TWO SUNDAYS INTO living with Nikki Fife, I already had a family tradition I bet I could make stick—even though we weren't technically a family yet, and might never be one if Nikki lost the baby. I stood in the kitchen, making waffles on a beat-up old waffle iron I bought at a garage sale the day we closed on the house, and I knew that if I made them again next Sunday, the tradition would be set in stone.

A lot could happen in a week, though. Nikki, thanks to a host of medical factors I couldn't even pronounce, had a crazily high chance of miscarriage. We weren't even sure we wanted to get married, and broke up four times between the day we found out she was pregnant and the end of her first trimester, when she was supposed to be out of the woods. Then we could finally talk about getting married, and she joked about waiting until she had a nice, big belly so she could really tick her mother off at the wedding. We went fantasy house shopping and narrowed it down to three neighborhoods, then five houses, then two.

We bought one of them, and before we could move in Nikki developed preeclampsia. High blood pressure, bloating, couldn't always see straight. She could die, the baby could die. Her ob-gyn prescribed bed rest and no more than two hours of activity a day, for no more than twenty minutes at a time. While I made the waffles Nikki decided to water the front porch plants, and she filled up the watering can only halfway so it wouldn't exceed her ten-pound carrying limit.

"Careful with that." I leaned toward the sink and kissed her.

"Heavy, I know." The front porch plants didn't actually need water, since until that morning it had been raining constantly for six days—unusual for Denver in May, but not unheard of. Sometimes raining in sheets, sometimes in drizzles, sometimes in big, heavy glops. I thought the plants got plenty of moisture from the air, but Nikki disagreed and I didn't argue with her. Didn't want to make her blood pressure spike and give her a stroke, which the doctor said was the worst-case scenario. Once she got done with the front porch plants she headed down the steps—I watched every move through the kitchen window—and went around the corner to check the hydrangeas, which I'd planted for her just before the rain. She moved gingerly and precisely, the way her doctor told her to, and didn't bend down much. When she smiled at me through the glass I knew I could learn to live with her, to make this house ours, to be her husband someday, to call a child mine.

"Rog-er?" she said ten seconds later, raising her pitch at the end like she thought there was trouble. It didn't necessarily mean there actually was any trouble, but because of the delicate pregnancy I had to act like it. Nikki stood frozen, hands on her belly, and stared at some fresh boot tracks in the soggy dirt by the side of the house. They were closer together than my tracks would've been, and smaller too. Plus I couldn't have made them—I hadn't set foot outside yet, and spent the whole night before listening to the rain with my hand on Nikki's belly.

"Rog-er?" she said again, and I unplugged the waffle iron. I slipped on my boots and headed outside, tracking the footprints until they stopped at our backyard fence. It had four slats missing, pried off and scattered on the ground.

"Is the back door still locked?" I asked her, and she nodded. This lowered the chance that whoever broke the fence had slipped inside our house to wait in a closet for his chance to kill us. The wood of the slats hadn't splintered much, which meant that whoever pried them off had done it carefully. Maybe even with a crowbar, which might be in his hands now as he gleefully waited in the backyard to break my skull.

"Go out through the back door," Nikki said. "See if anybody's in the yard first."

I nodded, then stepped straight through the fence. Preeclampsia or not, I just couldn't take that much paranoia. There was no maniac with a crowbar on the other side, just a three-foot-wide hole in the ground that somebody had filled back up in a hurry. I kicked at the wet, loose dirt and couldn't say anything for fifteen or twenty seconds.

"What is it?" Nikki finally asked.

"It's a hole. Would you get me the shovel, please?"

"Just a hole?"

"Yeah, just a hole. Covered back up."

Nikki poked her head through the fence and confirmed that it was just a hole. "Don't you think we would've heard it when they broke the fence?"

"Not with it raining like that."

"Who'd go out and dig a hole in the rain?"

"Somebody who has to bury stuff, I guess. Or dig it up."

"But at *our* house? Shouldn't we call the police?"

"The shovel, Nikki. Please. Then we'll figure out if we have to call the police."

She walked to the garage to get the shovel, which I could just as easily have fetched myself. But I needed to watch the hole, to protect Nikki from what was inside the hole. She passed the shovel through the fence and squatted down, disobeying doctor's orders, to watch me. The earth came up heavy, so wet it stuck to the metal. I had no idea how long I'd have to dig, or even what I was digging for. Two minutes later I hit something that made a hollow thunk.

"It can't be a body, can it?" Nikki asked.

"Impossible." Through the broken fence I saw her fingertips come together in front of her heart. I dug another minute and stopped to pull a thick black plastic bag out of the ground. From the way the dirt fell off it in clumps, I could tell it had been buried a lot longer than a night.

"Oh God," Nikki said, and her fingertips slid to her belly.

"You shouldn't watch if you're scared, Nik. Lean against something. Or go lie down."

"I'm fine. I'm leaning against the fence." But actually, she was still squatting. I opened the plastic bag and found a canvas army duffel inside, so clean you'd never guess it just came out of the ground. Inside that was a shiny red conga drum with a chink in its side from the point of my shovel.

Nikki stood and breathed in sharp through her nose. "It's damaged."

"I don't give a shit if it's damaged. Nobody should bury their junk in our backyard, okay?"

"But it was here before we were."

"I don't care when it was here. It's our house now, so it's going to the trash."

"Not the trash, please."

"Then Goodwill." I tried to say it soft, because I didn't want that baby to hear my voice and drop off the wall of Nikki's uterus. Didn't want her blaming me for that for the rest of my life, maybe longer. "It doesn't belong to us, Nik. It's not staying here."

Nikki dragged over a stray cinderblock and sat on it to watch me dig some more. I could feel her staring at the conga, worrying over the gash I put in it, and that pissed me off so much I dug harder. Then I thought of the baby again and dug softer. Then I thought about how I never asked for this life with her, never asked for this baby she wasn't even sure would last, and that made me dig harder again. Then I thought about my real dad, who'd never been anything but a wish to me and wasn't around to give me a damn bit of help getting ready to be a dad myself. That made me dig like a maniac until I ran out of breath.

"Anything else in there?" Nikki asked once I stopped.

"You mean the bag, or the hole?"

"Either."

I picked up the duffel, pushed it through the fence, and held it upside down—nothing. Then I went back to digging like a prisoner on a chain gang, and the next sound the shovel made was soft and heavy. I pulled out another black plastic bag with another army duffel inside it.

"Don't open it." Nikki jutted her hand through the fence like a school crossing guard's.

"But I have to open it, babe. How else will we know if it's a body or not?"

Nikki looked away and clenched her jaw. I shouldn't have made fun of her, I know, but what else can you do when the woman you love is more worried about a scratch in a complete stranger's conga than the fact that somebody is digging up her yard in the middle of the night? I untied the second duffel and lifted it off the ground with one hand.

"It's not heavy enough to be a body," I told her. "Plus it's got edges. Relax."

"I'll relax if you don't open it."

"I mean relax *here.*" I patted my belly and leaned toward the fence to give her my best, most loving smile. That was a hard smile for me to muster then, and for Nikki to give back. It was one of those moments as a couple when you grit your teeth and wordlessly tell each other, *We're going to get through this,* then go back to slogging across whatever river of shit you're stuck in.

I reached into the duffel and came out with a high school letterman's jacket from 1975, a year before I was born. Nice leather, with a football and the number 56 and a Denver North High School logo stitched onto it.

"Somebody from around here," I told her.

"You can't be sure of that."

"Yes, you can. Unless it's somebody who collects high school football jackets."

"Please don't take out any more." Nikki had this fear of permanently upsetting anything, of making changes to the universe that no one could ever undo. She was like those backpackers who try not to leave a trace that they ever passed through a place, except she felt that way about her whole life. I couldn't stand it. I dipped my hands into the duffel again and came out with a photo album covered in plastic wrap.

"How would you feel if somebody did that to you?" Nikki went on. "If you hid your things, and somebody else started pawing through them?"

"Well if I buried it in somebody else's backyard, I wouldn't expect a hell of a lot of privacy."

"Maybe Mrs. Gonsalves buried it." She was the last owner of the house.

"Mrs. Gonsalves was born in 1935. And she didn't play football."

"Maybe it was her son's, then."

"She has two daughters, no sons." Nikki ticked me off so much I put down the album and dug until my back spasmed. What the hell was she talking about, trying to lecture me about Mrs. Gonsalves when *I* was the one who made friends with her while we were getting ready to move in? When *I* took three truckloads of her junk to the dump for free? For a few seconds I didn't feel Nikki watching me — maybe she walked away, or maybe I just blotted her out of my mind while I dug. I didn't find any more black bags in the ground, so I stopped digging and unwrapped the plastic on the photo album. My fingertips couldn't feel a thing, that's how hard I was hoping the pictures inside would be of my real dad. Hoping he'd been watching me grow up all along, and buried the stuff in the backyard of my first house so he could show me who he was before I had a kid of my own.

"Huh," I said without wanting to when I saw the first page: an 8 x 10 of a man my height and build in a high school football uniform, number 56. He had the same bulb of a nose as me, the same bushy eyebrows, and right away I thought, *It's him.* But a billion other people on the planet had that nose, so I couldn't get too excited. He was there on the next page too, sitting behind the wheel of a white Corvette with a cigarette dangling out of his mouth. And on the page after that, bare-chested with a stack of two-by-fours on his shoulder. A builder, like me. A guy who probably dreamed about building his own house, like me.

"Roger?" Nikki, if she ever went away in the first place, was back. "What is it?"

"You didn't even want me looking at it before, hon. Why care now?"

"Don't get like that. Tell me what it is."

"It's pictures, okay? A family." I kept staring at the man with the two-by-fours, seeing if he could've been my father. Looking at the heft of his chest, the cut of his arms, the slope of his neck. The places he was strong and weak.

"Whose family?" Nikki asked. She wanted me to know who my real dad was as much as I did. I flipped the next page and saw the man again, this time with his arm around a Japanese-looking woman — not my mother, that's for sure. A few pages later the two of them were getting married, then they had a son who didn't look a damn thing like me. Then another son, then a daughter.

"I don't think it's mine." I slammed the album shut, wrapped it in its plastic, set it on the conga, and reached into the second duffel.

"Please stop," Nikki said, and I knew she'd start breathing shallow if I pulled anything more out of that bag. Knew I'd have to help her up to bed, where she'd stay for the rest of the day. "Put it all back in the ground. It's not ours to touch."

"So people should be able to bury whatever they want in our yard, is that what you're saying?"

"No, I didn't say that."

"Then why the hell should I bury this shit again?"

"Please, Roger." She leaned partway through the fence and reached a hand toward me. I could've taken two steps and grabbed it, but I stayed glued to my spot by the hole. "I want to have this baby. *Our* baby."

"Looking inside the bag isn't going to hurt our baby. Taking all this to Goodwill isn't going to hurt our baby."

"I *feel* like it is, okay? And I'm the one carrying it. That's somebody else's baby down there." She jabbed her finger at the hole. "Somebody's son who got killed in Vietnam or something."

"Vietnam was over before he got out of high school. He would've been too young to go."

But I couldn't keep arguing with her, couldn't risk hurting the baby, so I slid everything back into the duffels. That made Nikki feel like I could see things her way, which I knew she really needed right then. Life wasn't easy for her — a hell of a lot harder than for me, since she had to slog through this mess of ours with a baby inside her that could slip out any minute.

"Hey," I said as softly as I could once she got onto the porch. I stepped away from the hole so she'd know I wasn't poking through the bags anymore, then blew her a kiss. She started crying, wiped her eyes, and opened the front door. I tied up both duffels, wrapped them in their plastic bags like I was burying dead pets, and set them in the ground. Nikki waited a second with the screen door open, listening for the sound of me filling the hole back up, and I dug as loud as I could until I heard that door close. When I got back inside she was sitting at the dining room table, writing a letter with her best pen and paper.

Dear Sir:

We saw the hole in our backyard, and had to dig it to find out what was inside. We're sorry that we disturbed your things, but we only looked at the drum and a few of the pictures to make sure there was nothing to call the police about. We haven't called them, obviously, because they are nothing but family pictures, and we are the kind of people who respect family.

We know that you probably don't have a place to put these things, and appreciate the fact that you may have had them here before we moved in. But we are expecting a child, and it has been a difficult pregnancy, and the thought of people we don't know being around the house at night scares us. Even if they intend no harm.

If you need help finding another place for these things, we will be glad to assist you. We can even offer a bit of money toward a storage space. But we hope you can also understand our wishes and our needs as new owners of this house, and expectant parents.

Sincerely,

Nikki had already signed it. As I stood behind her reading the letter she held the pen out for me, lifting it back over her shoulder but not looking at my face.

"I'm not signing that." I wouldn't take the pen. "I think it's bullshit."

"Do you want somebody's curse?" she asked, half whirling around. "Somebody who sticks his family pictures in the ground and digs them out whenever he wants to see them? Do you want a man like that thinking bad things about our baby?"

I clenched my teeth—clenched my whole body, actually—to keep Nikki from feeling my anger. It was something I'd have to get used to as a father, I told myself, because I knew our baby would be soft and afraid like its mother. Always jumpy, boy or girl, because of how scared its mom was while she carried it. Always staring at my eyes when I walked into a room, ready to run away if it saw anything like anger in them.

But that was the wrong Roger—the one who never knew his real dad, who looked for traces of him in supermarkets, in movie theaters, in hardware stores, in other people's photo albums. The one who'd never cut it as a father, who'd run away at the first sign of trouble. I wanted to be a different kind of Roger, one who'd never make his wife and kid scared that he'd ditch them. Never leave his wife holding the bag, trying to explain why he ran out on her when he didn't even know himself.

So I smiled, took the pen, and signed her letter. Signed it like a duke, really, even using my middle name. When I went back to dot my *i* and cross my *t*, I pictured my hands reaching into a bag again — not into a buried duffel this time but into my black leather carry-on, and instead of taking things out I was putting things in. My passport, a plane ticket, my fake Rolex, the shaver cord I always forgot when I traveled. I put them in there for keeps, just like the person put that conga into the duffel, and the photo album, and the other things I didn't look at because I didn't want to make Nikki scared.

Screw that, I thought, putting the pen down on the table so gently I couldn't even hear it. Screw being afraid of her fear. I couldn't live like Nikki wanted me to, couldn't spend the rest of my life walking on eggshells to hide how I felt. Lying to myself and burning up inside, feeling bad just so my wife and kid wouldn't have to. I'd never make it, never be the kind of guy who stayed. It was in my genes like failure, like rot.

But then I heard Nikki breathing and everything inside me surrendered — I felt the word in my gut, felt the anger sliding through the bottoms of my feet and holding them to the floor. *Adore this woman,* I told myself in a voice I'd never felt before. It wasn't any softer or deeper than my usual voice, just not so worried about catching a bad wind and floating away like my dad did. *Worship this woman,* it said. *Honor this woman. Marry this woman.* I stroked the back of Nikki's neck, but her skin wouldn't yield to my fingers even though I'd signed the letter like she wanted me to.

"I'm leaving," I told her, though I had no idea those were the words that would come out of my mouth. I rested my hands on her shoulders and kissed the crown of her head.

"Leaving?" She put her hands over mine.

"That's what I said. That's what I meant."

But I didn't move. I looked down at Nikki's hands and pictured them filling up my carry-on with me. She put different things in it than I did — the braided belt my foster dad made for me when I was twelve, the red plastic bank in the shape of a goldfish that I'd found in the trash when I was seven and filled with pennies ever since. And then I caught myself putting Nikki's things into it, too. Her hair conditioner, one of the crime novels she was always reading, the little alarm clock she kept by her bed but never used. Like we were both leaving, or both packing up stuff to bury in somebody else's backyard.

My hands stopped for a minute, then Nikki's did. Stopped dead in mid-reach and shuddered, like they were from a movie that got jammed in the projector and was about to burn up. My real hands twitched a second under hers, but that's all. I couldn't tell if they were trying to push hers off, or flip themselves over so her palms would fall into mine.

"You're sure?" Nikki said. She looked back at me over her shoulder, but I closed my eyes before she caught them. I kept my mouth shut and pictured our hands again, just hanging there empty over that bag. I didn't know what they wanted, didn't know how long they'd stay there deciding. Until the baby came? Until we got married? As long as we stayed together, which maybe was forever? I couldn't breathe right, and the back of my neck started sweating, and then I felt Nikki's hand touch me where the sweat was coming fastest.

But that was impossible, because the real Nikki sat in front of me with her hands in mine, waiting for me to say something. She squeezed my fingers, and then both pairs of imaginary hands went back to packing up that carry-on. I put in the silver whistle I got when I coached youth football in college. Nikki put in a brooch in the shape of a penguin that her aunt gave her. I put in a piece of deer horn we found the first time we went camping. She put in a picture of the two of us dressed like it was 1975—carrying our baby that hadn't been born yet, and might never get to be.

A Story about Two
Prisoners

T HE WOMAN DOWNSTAIRS in apartment 1 understands many varieties of secret code thanks to her
private research into the covert actions of the Al-
lied Occupation in post–World War II Italy. She is convinced that
her upstairs neighbor is using a code developed during this period by Canadian soldiers who wanted to communicate with each
other without being understood by English-speaking soldiers
from other countries. This code was perfected by an intelligence
unit stationed in Naples and is known, at least officially, by fewer
than a dozen surviving veterans and their chosen designates.

The code consists of thumps and knocks, each pattern repre-
senting a single letter. Obscure letters such as *Q* and *X* are omit-
ted; *Z, K,* and *J* can be identified only by their relationship to
those around them. Vowel sounds are made with the open palm
(or palms), consonants with the knuckles. It is an extremely complex format to understand and re-create, but we must remember that the Canadian soldiers who developed it had nothing but
time. Years to sit idly in a foreign country, to try helping people
they could never know. Years to miss their homes and loved ones.

The woman downstairs is also convinced that the man above her, whom she occasionally sees by the main door of the apartment house wearing worn tweed coats several sizes too large, is sending her secret nighttime messages using this code. She sits in her kitchen, directly underneath his, and hears the thumps and knocks he makes on his table. She understands his words, but cannot comprehend the messages themselves.

conjure
inconsiderate
fulfillment
disgraced

wellspring
almighty
panic
deceit

years
forcefully
windows
grateful
peacemaker

placate
forcefully
inconsiderate
fulfillment

winter
windows
barren
wonder

Etc., etc., until the night is done. She types them into her laptop and prints them out at her office job on Friday afternoons after all her supervisors have gone home. She keeps the printouts in a notebook that once belonged to her brother, who disappeared when she was eight. She goes to sleep repeating the words to herself, trying to guess the next words in each series so she can discover their pattern and meaning.

Sometimes she sings them from her bed, hoping that the man above her—not much older than she is, and at least as shy—will hear his messages reflected back to him and know that he is not alone. Sometimes she wears the clothes she would like to meet him in: fine silks, a velvet scarf, a dress worn to a friend's wedding. Once or twice she has slept in those clothes and dreamed of waking up beside him. She hopes he will smile at her the next time they see each other by the main door of the apartment house, and that when the time comes, she will be brave enough to smile back.

Upstairs in apartment 3, the man sits at his kitchen table smoking clove cigarettes. He knows these are twice as deadly as anything else he can smoke, but they remind him of his college days: the last time he felt that his life had any significance beyond the limited sphere of his daily routine. At night he listens to music through noise-reducing headphones and drums along to it, his beats loud or soft depending on the tune and his mood. The music is always instrumental; the only voices involved are visceral cries and shouts in languages he does not recognize.

He wonders where his next home-cooked meal is coming from, and hopes it will come from the mousy little woman downstairs in apartment 1. She always has a smile for him in the hallway, despite his shabby clothing and frown. She could understand how he saw the world, the way his vision shifted with his mood. She could understand that there are people in the sky—all the people who have ever lived, and all those who ever will live—singing their hearts out and praying that at least a few of us will get it. Sometimes when he goes to sleep he swears he hears vague singing from the bedroom below, and wonders if the woman in apartment 1 is listening to the same songs.

After dinner, while she cleans up her kitchen, he sits at his table pounding out the rhythms of those songs. Many nights he drums along randomly to wild, antirhythmic jazz, rocking his body back

and forth as he pounds because it helps sing along with the people of the sky better. The people of the sky, who secretly control
all that goes on in the world. Who decide which of us must come
back to earth when we die, and which of us will be allowed to
leave. They sing:

> largesse
> dominion
>   accord
>
> fidelity
>   abnegate
> will
>   light
>   bearing
> seed
>
>   perfection
> splintered
>   condensed
> uproar
>   frigid
>
> squalor
>   redemption
>   perfection
>   only
> somewhere
>   without
>
> splintered
>   uproar
> abnegate
>   largesse
>   only
> somewhere
>   without

Etc., etc., until the night is done.

Meeting Grace

MY KID SISTER, Grace, is a real piece of work. Eyes made up dark, with half a pound of mascara on her, and a laugh like you'd hear from a hooker who leans through your car window when you're stuck in traffic. I've bailed her out and gone to bat for her so many times they ought to stick my chest full of medals and hang it up in city hall. Once she went hysterical and hid in my house to get away from her latest gym rat boyfriend, who came by an hour later to coax her home with twelve roses and two rottweilers. Another time she got arrested for stealing shaving cream at a drugstore—men's shaving cream of all things, when she didn't even have a boyfriend and was living in Mom and Dad's basement. I've been refused service in restaurants and beaten up at a bus stop once, all because she never had the sense to get out of Boston and go bother people somewhere else.

And all I wanted from Grace in return was good behavior when I brought her over to meet my fiancée. A totally reasonable thing, right? She had a new medication regimen that was supposed to stop her little episodes, and since there weren't any episodes lately I guessed she was taking the pills when they told her, not skipping days here and there as usual so she could feel independent. And

I knew that Priya, my fiancée, would keep Grace nice and calm when I finally got the two of them in one room. The only people who don't like Priya are the ones who don't like human beings at all. She's got those long, easy arms that sweep and sway and cool off everybody around her. They kept Grace cool through cheese and crackers, and even through the half glass of wine I gave her for trying so hard to act normal.

"Grace is sweet," Priya whispered to me in the kitchen while we tossed the salad and cut open the swordfish to see if it was cooked. "We could go to the museum. The museum of arts."

"Oh, she loves museums." I kissed Priya's Picasso nose and wondered how big a mistake I made by not telling her about Grace's problems before they met. It was almost criminal to let her get her hopes up too much, let her start thinking she might have a normal American sister-in-law who she could go to lunch with and shop with and talk about me behind my back with. Somebody who could settle her into Boston more, into the country more, and be there to help out when people talked at her too fast. Christ, it ate my guts to imagine those two out at some mall when Grace decided to get back into shoplifting. Priya would be nice and try to help her, like she tried to help everybody, but they'd both end up arrested and the feds would pull Priya's visa before she could even marry me.

That would never happen, I knew, but right then I was freaked out enough to picture it. Every way I looked at telling Priya about Grace and all her mental problems, it was a lose-lose situation. If I told her everything, then she'd be on her guard and distant, and Grace would know there was something wrong the minute she walked in the door—she's pretty good at picking up the vibe when people think she's crazy. If I didn't say anything, then Priya would have to figure Grace out all on her own. I chose to say nothing, because Priya has this way of figuring everything out by herself, of understanding things she couldn't say in English yet. She sees people once, and she knows them—it's how she gets through the world, and I love that about her.

But really I have to admit I was selfish, too, for keeping my mouth shut. Grace and I have the same genes, and I figured if I got lucky and Priya didn't see the bad side of Grace before the wedding, then she wouldn't look around for the bad side of me. And I'd get a break because I wouldn't have to look at my own bad side until later, either. Wouldn't have to stare at my own guts like I always do after Grace dumps her problems on me. Wouldn't have to tear up my own skin just so I could make sure I didn't have the same words stamped on my insides that Grace does, words I can never scratch out.

Sure, I was being selfish. But there wasn't time to explain all that to Priya, not when we were standing in the kitchen checking the swordfish. We had to bring it out and eat it and have a wonderful time with Grace, a nice calm family time, without anybody throwing wine glasses or crying about stuff Mom and Dad did twenty years ago.

"Ready?" I asked Priya, putting my arms around her skinny little waist and belly. I was talking to myself, sort of, trying to gear up for dinner with Grace. But that's not how Priya heard me, and she double-checked the fish.

"It's ready," she said. Once we plated up, Grace asked Priya to bless the food like she would in India, and she sang a song that almost made Grace cry. Priya's hands danced when she sang, so Grace got to see them plenty—the best hands in the entire world, with long bronze fingers that know just how hard or soft to touch everything. When it was over we clapped and Grace said she'd love it if we all had an Indian meal together someday, and sat on the floor like she did at an Indian restaurant in Cambridge one time. Or was that Japanese? She wasn't sure. But she was very charming and not visibly insane, which was all that mattered to me about her right then.

Grace said nice things about the engagement ring and asked what Priya did for work, what Priya did for fun. For a good long while Grace didn't have a reason in the world to bitch about me, or about our parents, or about how all the people who called her crazy were wrong and just didn't understand. But after a while the little green eel that was stuck inside her soul came out from under its rock and snapped at me like usual.

"Oh Jesus, Davey was a character." Grace rolled her eyes and started jabbering on about junior high, an awful time for both of us, and listed all the girls I kissed and dated back then. That was embarrassing enough, but she kept on going through high school, community college, one job after another. She told Priya about Jean, who ditched me a week before our wedding day when I was twenty-six. Told her about Barbara, who I almost married last year.

But some of the stuff wasn't real, that's the problem. I mean, they were all real women I knew, but the stuff Grace said I did never happened with half of them. Some of them were women I told her I liked, but never even asked out. Or women I kissed but never slept with, or women I slept with but never asked to marry me. She jumbled them all up and it made me look like I'd sleep with anybody too stupid to run away. If I straightened Priya out on every little detail, then I'd look too defensive and Grace would stick it to me even more. So I figured if I let Grace run all the way to the end of her chain, let her keep bullshitting until she wasn't making sense anymore, then Priya would see how nuts she was and all those lies would add up to nothing.

"Let me tell you something about Davey," Grace told Priya, stabbing a tomato with her fork. Her leg swung at me under the table like it always used to when we lived with Mom and Dad, arcing higher each time and looking for my knee. "He knows something about women, he really does. You can tell that, can't you?"

"Yes?" Priya smiled, but she could barely follow the conversation.

"Oh, I love them all." I gave Grace a big smile, bunching up my cheeks like Dad used to when he wanted Mom to shut up. I knew what I was doing, knew how to push Grace's buttons and piss her off enough to make her start screaming and leave. I turned to Priya and kept that smile up for a second, then let my cheeks fall and my eyes droop down as far as they'd go. *I'm sad, see?* I was trying to tell her. *My sister hurts me.* But Priya didn't get it. She was too young to see past Grace's downtown style and museum promises, and not American enough yet, either. She cocked her head and squinted at me like I had the problem, not Grace.

"He's not lying, kiddo." Grace's foot thunked against the bottom of the table and she stopped swinging it—she couldn't reach me unless she slid all the way down in her chair, and even she wasn't shameless enough for that. She flung her hair to the side, keeping hold of Priya's eye. "He loves every one of them, you'll find out."

Priya sat up and let her fork drop to the plate with a chunk of fish still on it. She swept her hair off her ear just like Grace did, and I'm almost positive she didn't even know she was doing it. That's the great thing about Priya and the bad thing, I guess. She's so natural, so free, but she can't tell when somebody like Grace is playing her.

I wished I had more time to think about Priya then, or even pay more attention to her feelings. But I couldn't, because the disaster with Grace I wanted to avoid was staring at me from across the table, like a scene in a movie I forgot I wrote. The scene where the woman I want to marry gets her head all flipped around by my crazy little sister, who deep down inside knows she's more like a wife to me than anybody I'll ever find. Who wants to dredge up the whole Mom and Dad thing and rebuild it in my living room, brick by brick, with her and me trapped in the middle. That's why she keeps on making me save her. I even told one of her shrinks that, and he said, Yes, oh definitely yes. But he couldn't do a damn thing to change it.

I looked at Priya and rubbed my fingers on my forehead, the same spot where she dabs that red dot whenever I take her to see her aunt. *If you can just get through dinner, honey,* I wanted to tell her. *Just let stuff slide past you until Grace is gone, then I'll tell you everything.* But it didn't happen that way. Priya nodded at Grace, trying to make sense of that crap she heard about me and all those women, and then she looked at me like I was supposed to fight back and call my sister a liar. But I couldn't fight back, couldn't look either one of them in the eye right then.

"I'm sorry," Priya said to Grace real slow. "My English. I don't know what you say." She stroked her throat like she always did when she couldn't follow a conversation, but I knew it wasn't the language that bothered her. It was the people. It was us.

"Just wait," Grace told her. "When you move in here and say you want to go to this restaurant or that restaurant, he'll say, 'Oh no, the food's no good there.' But what he really means is some woman he used to screw works there, or likes to eat there, and he's scared to show his face 'cause he was such a shit when he dumped her."

"Grace doesn't usually get like this unless she's had a bit more to drink," I told Priya as calmly as I could.

"I don't need booze to tell the truth!" Grace snarled like a dog does when you try to steal its food. Priya stared straight at her, and she had to know my sister was crazy by then. Had to know.

"Priya, honey?" I turned and put my hand on hers, showing Grace nothing but the back of my head. "You need to under-stand—"

"*What* does she need to understand?" Grace tapped her fin-gernails on the edge of her plate. She knew I hated that. "What, Davey? Tell her."

"She needs to understand that her future sister-in-law has not always been mentally *stable*." I turned to Grace and folded my hands together on the placemat, talking to her like I was twenty years older instead of two. Very calm, very dignified, and very straight-backed, like the *Mayflower* bluebloods our whole family wished we were. "She needs to understand that Grace takes pills to keep her from doing this to everybody she meets. She needs to understand that Grace has been sent to the nuthouse in Mattapan for observation *twice*." I looked at Priya and asked, "You know what a nuthouse is, right?" and when she nodded I didn't worry so much about losing her anymore.

"Observation doesn't mean anything," Grace spat back. She sat up just as straight and blueblood as I did, but her fingers kept tapping at the plate. "They could stick *you* in the nuthouse for observation too."

"But *I* don't steal things. *I* don't scratch people's faces in line at the bank. *I* don't throw rocks at police cars." I leaned forward so deep that both women's faces were above me, and I could feel my own face tighten up and get hard like it did only when I had to shut Grace up. I hated having to do that. What I really should've done right then was disappear, left the room. Because if I disappeared then maybe Priya could've calmed Grace down a little, could've cooled the whole room off with her sweepy arms and those soft, perfect fingers. I watched those fingers, calm and brown and quiet against the silver of the tablecloth, but couldn't bring myself to touch them.

"I'm sorry, honey," I said to Priya instead. "I should've told you about Grace, but I thought she'd be okay tonight."

"Don't you love it how he calls you honey?" Grace rolled her eyes at the ceiling. "Think how many other women in this town he's called honey. That's why he had to go get a foreign girl — not that there's anything wrong with being foreign, don't get me wrong. But he needs you because you won't understand how people look at him, or the little digs they make behind his back. You know what I mean, don't you? You're not a dumb girl."

Grace kept her eyes locked on Priya's until she was sure her words got through, then started nodding. Priya nodded back and didn't look away from her at all, except to shoot a half-trusting glance at me with one eye.

"I think we've had our little visit, Grace," I said, knowing the worst wasn't over. She had a way of throwing a scene that made it look like everybody's fault but her own, and it drove me so crazy my finger shook when I pointed at the door. Grace ignored me completely, another thing she was good at.

"Priya, honey," she said. "You've got to know something about him before you marry him. He's going to turn into his father one day, out of the blue. It'll just happen without any warning, and there's no turning back. He can't help himself. He'll choke the life out of you, just like his father choked the life out of me. He'll tell you who you can be and who you can't be."

"Grace?" I stood up steady, like I was balancing a bowl of acid on my head, and dropped my napkin onto her plate. "I think you're finished eating now. I think you're ready to leave."

"I'm not finished eating, *Dad!*" She grabbed the napkin and whipped it against my chest, then started pounding the table. *"Dad! Dad! Dad! Dad! Dad! Dad! Dad!"*

Finally I couldn't do anything but get my arm around her neck and my hand over her mouth. That's the only way you can shut Grace up sometimes. She held her breath and looked over at Priya, who kept her eyes on her own plate. I barely looked at her myself because all I wanted was to get Grace out of my house before the wreck got any bigger. Priya was just an idea to me right then, and if she decided not to marry me she'd never be anything more than that.

"You're okay," I whispered in Grace's ear, like I saw an EMT do to her once when she got caught stealing and the cops had to hold her down. "You're fine now. You're breathing easy."

And after a minute or so—a whole minute when I couldn't look at Priya, when Priya barely existed for me—Grace finally started breathing normal again. When I took my hand away from her mouth she was calm, like all that stuff never happened.

"I could've bitten you," she said. "But I wanted to be nice to your fiancée." Then Grace got up, looked at Priya, and said, "I'm sorry, honey. You'll learn."

Thank God it was summer and Grace didn't have a jacket to get or anything. In ten seconds she was out the door, whistling and swinging her little white pocketbook behind her. Priya stood up and watched me like she was waiting for me to tell her the next thing to do. I had no idea what they did with crazy people in India. Maybe they don't even have them. Maybe they send them out in the woods to die. I couldn't get the words lined up in my mouth, though I felt like telling Priya how I'd understand if she decided to give the ring back. And I wanted to tell her that if she stayed, if she was still my fiancée, then I'd tell her Grace's whole life story from start to finish, so she'd know the kind of family she was marrying into.

But I couldn't say any of that. I sat in Grace's chair and rested my forehead on my thumbs.

"I'm sorry," I told Priya again, barely looking at her. "I should've told you about Grace."

"She has problems."

"Yeah. Big problems. I made a mistake."

"I'm cleaning up now." Priya tiptoed into the kitchen with her head down, all the sweep and sway gone from her. At least her voice sounded like it always did, soft and round and unbroken. She could see how Grace was, and how long I'd been trying to straighten the kid out. But Priya wouldn't poke around in the muck of Grace's life, wouldn't dredge up old stuff and make me talk about it every day and night, because that wasn't her way of doing things. Priya's way was to let me be, and let Grace be too. Just move on, look at what was in front of her instead of behind her. *I'm cleaning up now*—isn't that what she said? Didn't that sum up everything wonderful about her, everything I loved about her? Well it did to me right then, so I decided I'd clean up too.

Move forward, Dave, I told myself while I gathered up more dishes than I could really carry. *Keep moving forward.* I had to shoulder the kitchen door open because my arms were too full. It smacked loud against the counter and I saw this look on Priya's face like I'd never seen before—not sure what was coming through that door at her, not sure I'd stay the same Dave she thought she knew. When I saw that face I put down the dishes and dropped to my knees, just like on the night I proposed to her.

"You're leaving me, aren't you?" I asked her. I took her left hand in both of mine and stroked her ring. I wanted her to tell me *No, I'm staying, can't you see I'm meant to be your wife?* Wanted her to run her fingers through my hair and tell me *You're not Grace, you don't have to worry about being like Grace.*

But when Priya didn't say anything back to me, I said, "Aren't you?" again, and that was my big mistake. She must've thought I wanted her to leave, because that's exactly what she did. Put the salad bowl by the sink, rinsed her hands off, and left.

And maybe I wanted her to, who knows. But I still think Priya would've married me if I hadn't said "Aren't you?" that second time. Every night I squeeze myself down tight enough to fit inside her skin so I can move like her, breathe like her, sweep my arms through the air real soft and feel the world like her. Every night, even now, Grace or no Grace.

Faster

FOUR TIMES IN MY LIFE, starting when I was seventeen, I've dreamed that my brother, Don, has crawled into my mind to try fixing it, but failed. He always gets stuck inside me too, because I never know he's there and lock him in by mistake. In the dreams my mind is this big rectangular thing, about the size of a Coke machine, with flashing colored lights all around it. It's not fancy, but it's a happy-looking gadget, the kind I figure all sorts of people would smile at if they saw it standing on a street corner. But it must have had problems, or Don wouldn't be crawling inside it and working on it all the time. And I guess I must like him being in my mind, because in the dreams I can barely tell the difference between having him in there and not. I keep going on with my life like he's not even around, keep humming along just the same even though he's got the wrenches out, even though he's rerouting all the wires.

By the end of every dream, Don's slumped in a corner of my mind crying with his face in his hands, hopeless because he can't fix me. This is where dream and reality part ways. Don never admits defeat like that—he never has losses, only temporary setbacks. Whenever he runs into a problem, he has the entire history of human consciousness at his disposal to make him aware of every possible solution. He's a smart guy, a professor all the way. Once he bragged that there wasn't a wall in his house that could hold all his publications lined up spine to spine, and he told me this two days in a row like he'd double-checked it in the middle of the night. Don is a certified genius who doesn't even have to teach anymore because he's always getting fellowships and grants to send him to Italy and Iceland and Bulgaria and Bolivia. (Not a bad deal for me, because I get to housesit when he's gone.) The grant he's on now gave him a quarter million—not $250,000 but a quarter million, that's an important distinction to Don. This was just enough to maintain Rafaela, the ex-model and medieval architecture scholar wife he acquired during one of his semesters in Rome. Not bad for an orphan Polack from the wrong side of the tracks, he likes to say whenever money comes his way.

"Not bad at all," I say back to him, like an admiring baby brother should. And I've been a great baby brother to Don all along. I worshipped him when I was a kid, tried to be like him and never hated his guts even when I realized I couldn't live up to his standards. I always had the same basic skills as Don, the same "keen intellect and penetrating wit" (he wrote that about himself once for a book jacket), but never enough drive to put me over the top. There was potential, always potential. My dissertation might get published someday, my adjunct gigs might roll into a tenure-track job.

"But only if you *let* yourself," Don tells me whenever he feels like bugging me about my damn potential. "*Let* yourself, that's the thing." It makes me wonder if what he's really looking for inside that Coke-machine mind of mine is the off switch for the little gizmo that keeps making me stop myself—let's call it my turbo-inhibitor. Don keeps flicking it off so I can't stop myself from going into turbo like him, but it won't work because the wires coming in and out of it are all screwed up. One day he'll get those wires straight, damnit, and when he flicks that switch I'll jump into turbo faster than anybody thought I could. Though not quite as fast as Don can, of course. Let's not get carried away.

• • •

While my big brother enjoys all the perks of the international professorial jet set, I toil among the thronging mass of low-paid itinerant lecturers and adjunct instructors who do all the dirty work in academia. In the eight years I've lived in Denver I've taught at nine different colleges, none of which will ever hire me for real. I teach whenever they tell me to, but try to keep my Wednesday afternoons free so I can have my ritual weekly lunch with Don —assuming he's not on a jet or being entertained by the intellectual elite of some foreign country. Wednesday lunch is my chance to hear Don talk about the world's latest psychic crises. There's always something wrong with the world, he thinks, never with the way we live in it. He and I part ways there; but after eight years of Wednesday lunches, whether we part ways or not has no bearing on how thoroughly Don lectures me.

"It starts with basic emotional *pain*," he started out this week. "The pain of living that your body experiences from being too fully in the world without necessarily wanting to be in it at all. The pain seeps through your nervous system, through every part of your body and every one of your senses, and it *floods* your brain. But the brain isn't configured to feel it as pain, you understand? That's an evolutionary self-defense mechanism. We aren't *able* to take the pain straight because it would *kill* us, just kill us. So we turn those neural impulses into words, into complaints, into demands we make on ourselves and the ones we love. We come up with formulas to turn the pain into words and dispel it, like the words are some kind of witchcraft that can turn *back* on the source of the pain and *change* it. If we don't turn that pain into words, then it simply sits in the body and turns into disease— like a question that's absolutely *un*answerable."

Don's a very smart guy, like I said. I have a master's in philosophy and a Ph.D. in art history, and I don't know what the hell he's talking about half the time. I love listening to him because he's my big brother, and I especially love the way he *italicizes* things with his *voice*. It's like everything he says is already in a book, waiting to be pored over by browbeaten, overeager grad students.

"Fascinating," I said as I watched a couple two tables over, giggling and stealing forkfuls of food from each other's plates. I've watched them before because they're regulars, like us, at Le Central, a nice, cheap French place halfway between Don's house and my apartment. Don lets only one waitress serve us—her name is something Romanian that's torturous even for a genius like him to pronounce, but she makes everybody call her Jasmine.

"But you see what I'm saying, don't you?" Don started in on his usual salad, romaine lettuce with hazelnuts and pâté. "We're not *designed* to process our pain. We *instinctively* assign it different manifestations. Art, politics, hatred."

"Yes, I see." I stuffed a big slice of mushroom into my mouth and wondered, like I did each Wednesday afternoon, if Don's latest sermon on the poor condition of the world was a thinly veiled poke at me and my half-fulfilled life. But I didn't think about it too long, because my brain isn't designed for that kind of thinking. It's *designed* to *deflect* the pain. Instead, I told him—

"I just read that Vladimir Lenin had horrible bunions."

"Really?" Don cocked his head like he always does at a fact he hasn't heard before. There were so few of them, I guess, that he always had to look them up and down when he met them.

"Sometimes it got so bad he needed help getting down the stairs."

"You're bullshitting me." He tried to stare me down and make me crack.

"Why would I do that?" I said, and shrugged. We've been playing this game for thirty years, and I'll never get tired of trying to stump him. Of trying to make him look like the gullible one.

"Because you're *you*. Because it's your nature."

"You think I'm constantly bullshitting you?"

"Yes," he said, "as always. I'm going home to read up on Lenin now."

Don put his knife and fork at the four o'clock position on his plate, which Rafaela had taught him was a signal that he'd finished eating. He dabbed his mouth ever so delicately with a napkin, pushed back his chair, and delivered the same stiff wave he always gave me when our lunches ended.

"Don't go," I said, holding out my hand to stop him. I knew better than to say "Almost got you!" or "Had you going!" or anything like that, because if I did Don would get his dander up and insist that I never had him stumped for a second.

"So you *are* bullshitting me," he snorted instead.

"Yes, I'm bullshitting you. I'll never do it again."

"Right!" Don laughed in a half circle around him, as if everybody at the nearby tables had listened in on our discussion and cared deeply about Lenin's imaginary bunions. Then he sat back down, put the napkin on his lap again, and chewed a mouthful of salad down to mush with a glint in his eye that said I'd never truly get the better of him as long as I lived. I smiled at him, thinking up something completely anti-intellectual to say that would permanently destroy all his hopes for me. Because I was sick of Don hoping for me. Sick of him looking down on everything I did that he wasn't capable of doing anymore, and maybe never had been. Laughing in public, flirting just to make people smile, dancing with people you don't know. Fucking people you don't know. I licked salad dressing off my fingers and watched a skinny girl in an orange minidress as she walked to the ladies' room. I felt like talking about her ass in front of Don just to piss him off, to prove I was completely déclassé and beyond his help, unfixable no matter how many times he crawled into my mind. But he noticed me looking at the girl, because he makes it his job to notice everything I do.

"So how are things going with this new girl?" he said. "She's another art history type, right?"

"I can't seem to get anything else with my résumé." I'd dated three art history women in a row, a grad student and two fellow adjuncts, since I broke off my engagement with Janet — the woman I'll probably spend the rest of my life kicking myself for not marrying. But Janet was another thing Don would never understand, a pain in my hips and my ribs that traveled the neural pathways to my brain, turning into a set of words I could never say to him. "I'm going to see her after lunch. She lives by Washington Park."

"A DU girl?" Don raised an eyebrow in half approval. He and Rafaela had friends who lived in Washington Park and taught at Denver University. "Is she tenure track?"

"No, starving adjunct. She went to Yale too, a couple years behind me." Don nodded and I kept going, since I'd said all the right things so far. "Her name's Fumiko. She's Japanese."

"Japanese!" He raised both eyebrows this time. I remembered how much Don was obsessed with Japanese culture as a teenager, the pomp and the tradition and the elegance. He said the Japanese made the British royal family look like apes. He said, "As Japanese poetry reached its apex, the Germans were cutting their veins open to bleed at the moonlight." He was fourteen then. A genius already.

I couldn't tell Don that Fumiko grew up with an American mother in upstate New York, where her father was an unglamorous electrical engineer, or that she spoke just a little Japanese and read not a single word of it. Couldn't tell him that she didn't have a commanding knowledge of *ukiyo-e* painting and Noh theater. Couldn't say that the only truly Japanese thing in her apartment was an autographed handprint of a sumo wrestling star. It was easier to let Don have his own delusions about Fumiko and imagine the role she'd play in my life when I married her. For Don she'd be the quiet little mouse I needed, someone who'd make me green tea and read haikus whenever my brain smoked from too much abstract thinking.

"So do you think you could marry her?" he asked me out of nowhere.

"It's been two months, Don. We hardly know each other."

"You know what I mean. Not do you *want* to right now, but *could* you, at some theoretical point in the future?"

I shrugged my shoulders and wobbled my head from side to side. It was a lukewarm response, but that's how I felt about Fumiko. Don imitated me, but he rolled his eyes when he did it.

"Why are you so obsessed about marrying me off?" I said.

"I'm not obsessed. You're the one who wants to, you just haven't found the right girl."

"Sure, I found her. I didn't have the balls to pull the trigger, that's all."

Don ignored my reply. I made my eyes as sad and misty as I could, hoping this would get him to feel guilty about making me break up with Janet. Technically, he didn't *make* me—he never told me I should dump her—but he always asked me skeptical, complicated questions about the life I planned to live with her. About the little house in the mountains, about the babies, about the stained-glass shop we wanted to start together. He never approved of our schemes because he never understood her. She was too slippery and real for him to ever get his sticky little mind around.

So ten months ago I made the biggest mistake of my life and broke off our engagement, and when I told Don he patted me on the back and said, "It's for the best." He's never said anything bad about Janet, but then again he'd never showed any *joy* for me like I wanted him to. Your brother's in love, I always felt like telling him. Show some fucking *joy!* But now it's too late to say that.

"So you think Janet was the right girl for you?" He pursed his lips and shook his head in that barely perceptible Don way. "You're back to that, I see."

"I'd be happier married to her than I am alone, wouldn't I?"

"Let's face it." Don held his fork in the air, two globs of pâté dangling from the tines. "I know you loved her, but she didn't exactly fit into the scheme of your life. So you tried to fit into the scheme of hers, and it didn't work out. Face reality, Nick. It never would have, no matter what you did."

But Don was wrong. The life we wanted was halfway between what Janet had before I came along and what I had before she came along, and neither one of us would have bent over backward for the other. On the way to Fumiko's apartment I looked for Janet's face through what must have been a hundred car windows, trying to remember it exactly. After a while you forget your ex-lovers' faces, even if you have pictures of them to remind you. Forget how they move, how they reflect light, the electricity you feel when they're nuzzling yours.

That slow kind of forgetting happened with almost every girlfriend I'd ever had, but Janet's the only one I still keep looking for. Most of the time she's sitting in the corner of my left eye, waiting for me to turn and look at her so she can smile and remind me of everything we could have had. I'll catch a glimpse of her for a second, exactly how she used to look, but when I try to fix both eyes on her, it turns out she's another woman. Sometimes a woman who doesn't look a thing like Janet. And then the memory of her face is gone too—I can't get the lips right, the nose right, the eyes right. Pretty soon it feels like she's slipped away for good.

Well I kept looking for Janet at every red light until I got sick of women's faces altogether. Sick of the pouty militant little mouths, of the repressed beady eyes that couldn't look at anybody, of the slack cooler-than-thou jaws. Theoretically I might see Janet for real because she still lived in Denver somewhere—I never ran into her, though, since all our mutual friends despised me. But no matter how many car windows I looked into, none of the faces I saw turned into Janet's. Not even the ones with the same cheekbones, or the same chin.

"Not you," I said to one of them through the glass. "Not you either," I told another. *What would you do if you found her, Nick?* I asked myself, but it was Don's voice I heard. *Jump out of the car and ask her to marry you again just so you could dump her again? Of course you wouldn't. Face reality.*

I closed my eyes at the light on Broadway and First and thought I saw Janet coming out of the Mayan Theater wearing the gray winter coat I bought her our first Christmas together. It wasn't Janet, and it wasn't even winter, but I took that anonymous woman coming out of the Mayan and bundled her up for a storm. Gave her the fur-lined black gloves I got Janet on our second Christmas, plus the purple beret I bought her on our first real date—a cheap rag I got for ten dollars at a cart downtown because she felt a cold coming on. She wore it all the time after that, even though she had better hats.

And that's when I got Janet's face back again, just for a second. Didn't have to look through any car windows for it, either. I just saw it hanging in front of me plain as day, tucking a little wisp of hair back under that purple beret and laughing at something I said. Something stupid and utterly nonprofessorial, utterly nongenius.

Fumiko's apartment was on Pearl Street a block up from Sushi Den—the best sushi in Denver, but she hated the stuff passionately and I couldn't get her to eat there no matter how much I tried. In Don's mind, that alone would have disqualified her from being truly Japanese. There's an antique shop right underneath her place, and the owner must have read my mind because every time I went to visit her he was out by his front door smoking a cigarette. We waved to each other, then I opened up the outside door with the spare key Fumiko gave me because her buzzer didn't work. It wasn't a gesture of trust or affection, but a mere acquiescence to practicality.

"Hel-lo!" I called up the stairs extra loud in lieu of a buzzer. Fumiko and I hadn't really jumped each other in a couple weeks —we had sex, sure, but it was very deliberate—so when she opened the door I threw my arms around her and kissed her before she could even talk. She wouldn't let her mouth open up, and pulled away instead.

"I've been eating cheese," she said. "No frenching, please."

"I've been eating it too. Doesn't bother me."

But Fumiko kept backing off until I grabbed her again and nibbled on her neck. She laughed when I pressed my hips against hers because I was half-hard already.

"Something on your mind?" Fumiko said, and she let me unbutton her jeans. Fumiko's more about her brain than her body, and usually if I want to get her real wet I have to go down on her. But she won't kiss me after that, and I felt like kissing her a lot that day. So I guess I was lucky because when I pulled off her underwear she was plenty wet. I nibbled at her thighs—big, ripe American thighs, none of this coy Japanese stuff that gets Don so excited. We threw couch cushions on the floor and got right down to it. I kept kissing her so she wouldn't talk, and pretty soon she forgot about the cheese and kissed me back. Eventually we went into the bedroom where the condoms were and I finished up from behind, which Janet never minded and sometimes even liked. I don't think Fumiko had done it that way before, because she let out some weird-sounding grunts and didn't quite know how to relax. I leaned forward and rolled us onto our backs and started stroking between her legs, not sure if she'd come yet.

"I'm fine," she said, patting my arm away. "Thank you."

I stopped stroking and kissed her again because I didn't believe in saying "Thank you" or "You're welcome" after sex. It was something two people did together, not a favor you gave and expected somebody else to return. We held hands when our mouths started to feel too cheesy for kissing, then fell half asleep until Fumiko looked at the clock and freaked out. She taught at three, which meant she had half an hour to clean herself up and get to DU. She turned on some music and raced around the apartment, showering and getting all her things together while I threw my condom in the trash and flipped through a book of World War I drawings by Otto Dix—hardly the stuff you want to look at naked after sex, but what the hell. It was sitting there on the coffee table, waiting for somebody to look at it.

"I'm driving you in, right?" I asked Fumiko at the height of her panic. She looked like she was asking herself why I was still there. "Then I'm picking you up after class, and we're going to the gym?"

"Exactly," she said. It was a cold, precise answer, not the kind you give to somebody who was just coming inside you ten minutes before. I dressed in seconds and kept looking at the Otto

Dix book until Fumiko said she was ready, then we headed out and waved to the nameless guy smoking his cigarette in front of the antique shop. I drove Fumiko to DU with time to spare—I tried to stop myself from looking for Janet in car windows, but couldn't—and she gave me a real kiss when I stopped to let her out. She even grabbed my hand and put it between her plump American breasts.

"See you at five-thirty," she told me. "Here."

"Here," I said back. There was something else that wanted to come out of my mouth, and Fumiko could tell. She opened the car door and cocked her head at me.

"What?" she asked.

"Nothing." But we could both tell that was bullshit.

"Come on, tell me." She grabbed her briefcase and nudged me in the arm with it.

"So what do you think?" I said, shrugging. "Do you want to get married?"

"To you?" Fumiko practically fell out of the car.

"No, to the next guy who smiles at you. Of course to me."

"Is that a proposal? Now?"

"No, it's a question. It's theoretical. People ask theoretical questions all the time. You don't have to answer it."

"Thanks." Fumiko stepped out onto the curb and pointed at her building. "I'm not ready for this conversation. It's a little heavy before a class, don't you think?"

"Oh, I'm just fantasizing aloud. Can't I do that?"

"I guess so." Fumiko furrowed her eyebrows at me and walked away. She turned back twice on her way to her classroom, but I think it was just to see if I was still there looking at her. And I was. Just staring at her swinging briefcase, watching her get smaller and smaller.

Fumiko had me drop her off at home after class, and we never made it to the gym that night. She didn't want to acknowledge my question, and I didn't want to acknowledge that there was anything wrong with asking it, so it was a weird drive back. On

Friday afternoon we were supposed to go out for dinner and a visit to Boulder, where some experimental film buddy of her department head was having a show. By six-thirty she hadn't swung by my place as planned, and I figured she was either stalling or bailing. So I called.

"I don't think I can make it," she said with the same voice she had before we started sleeping together. Cold, but with the promise of getting warmer someday.

"Are you feeling okay?"

"Fine. Maybe a little freaked about Wednesday."

"You mean about the getting married thing?"

"Of course. I've been proposed to before, I've just never had anybody say it so . . . offhand. So casually, like it didn't matter."

"I wasn't proposing. It was a theoretical question, like I said."

"Then it was even weirder."

The line went silent for a while, and Fumiko threw some food together in her kitchen. Her microwave said *beep-beep*.

"Who proposed to you before?"

"A couple guys. A guy named Tom, a guy named Greg, a guy named Vince."

"That's three, that's more than a couple. How did they ask you?"

"I don't see how it matters, Nick."

"It does if you turned them down. Maybe you'd turn anybody down. Maybe you're not ready for it."

"I think I have to go," she said, and hung up. That was good, because the next thing I would have asked her is if she wanted to have my babies. Then I figured out a great way to piss Don off —knock up some twenty-year-old student of mine and marry her right away, then show up with her at Le Central some Wednesday. Just walk in flashing our wedding rings—damn, that would piss him off! He'd probably take her aside and offer to pay for an abortion just to save us all. To save the great Jankowski name from somebody who sold curtains for a living like Janet did, or filed papers at an office all day long.

"You like that, Don?" I yelled into my kitchen, where I pictured him swirling around a glass of my wine and deciding, after much deliberation, that it was worthy of his palate. "You'd love it if I showed up with some knocked-up bimbo, wouldn't you?"

But fuck Don, I said to myself. It's always what *Don* thinks and what *Don's* going to do. Sometimes I wish I had another brother, let's call him Ron, who didn't need to get inside my head at all. He'd be older than Don, and I'd hardly know anything about him — maybe he was just a half-brother I grew up not knowing I had. He worked with regular people instead of intellectual snobs, so he didn't worry about fixing my mind at all. He'd put his ear next to the machine and hear it running smooth, then ask it a few random questions. Maybe the answers it spat out didn't make complete sense, but they were in the ballpark and that's all you can really ask from a mind. They're imperfect machines, and you have to cut them some slack.

Anyway I could call Ron and tell him how I'd screwed up with Fumiko, and he'd help me laugh it off. He'd probably tell me to get away from the professor types for a while, and just fling around with an ex-student or two. We'd set up a time for racquetball and I'd start doing some pushups and squats so maybe I could finally beat him — Ron always won that third game because he had more staying power, but I was pulling closer. And he never gloated over winning, because he earned it every time and was too tired to boast about it. Not like Don, who played little head games nobody else knew the rules to and then treated you like an idiot because you couldn't beat him.

But Ron didn't exist, and I couldn't call Don about Fumiko without hearing some big, admonishing lecture. Oh well. Part of me wanted to whack my phone off the kitchen table and against the wall, but I wasn't that rash of a person. Instead I poked it forward a few millimeters at a time with my index finger. Nudge, nudge. Dink, dink. It was an old-fashioned metal phone, not one of those portable plastic jobs, and it made a nice loud noise when it finally crashed to the floor.

· · ·

My favorite treadmill at my gym is the one they stuck in the corner to save space, the one almost nobody uses because it means being alone. The other treadmills look out on the Sixteenth Street Mall, a pedestrian zone the city of Denver put in to make the town seem more urban than it really is. Mine faces nothing but an employees-only door the bosses use when they have to file paperwork or chew somebody out. When I'm on it, I don't feel like I'm in Denver at all—I could be in Alabama, East Timor, Saskatchewan. There's no reality there except for the one I put in front of me.

Usually I jog at 5.0 or 5.2 miles an hour, but that night I clomped along at 4.3, thinking how good it was that Fumiko would never be my wife. She was cold, fussy, and had bad taste. Who else in the world thinks Gaugin is overrated, and likes Kirchner better than Klee? And people should smile at somebody they just made love to, not stare at them on the couch like they wandered into the wrong apartment. When Don asked me about her again next Wednesday I could say I'd told her a tasteless joke about the Japanese, and that she'd stopped returning my calls. Then I could smear pâté on my face like war paint, and confess to him that I was a flawed human being with no hope of salvation unless he crawled into my mind and fixed my turbo-inhibitor once and for all. He'd be glad to hear that finally. I'd tell him about my Coke machine dreams, and he'd nod like he'd been sending them to me every night for the past thirty years.

Anyway I ran like crap—my feet couldn't keep an even rhythm on the treadmill, so they both took turns pounding heavier than the other. Or I'd slip back from the pace, then jump ahead and end up bumping the rail. I almost let myself fall, so I could make a big scene and wallow in self-pity awhile.

"What's wrong with him?" all the people at the gym would say. Some would laugh at me, some would try to help, some would call an ambulance and disappear immediately. Falling down in public would have been a good way to tell the world how tired I was of being Nick Jankowski. To tell the world he needed to shed his skin and become somebody new—sort of like a movie star going into rehab, but in a minuscule, minor-league way.

But that day, Nick Jankowski couldn't get out of his skin so easy. He could get out of it only by shedding it, running out of it while it was still on his body, and he could do that only if he went faster than the old skin had ever taken him before. So he jabbed at the pace button, speeding up until he felt the pain of each step shoot up from his shins to his hips. He broke into a sprint like a kid alone in an empty field with nothing to stop him, not even his own idea of how fast he could run.

Up to 7.5? Piece of cake. Up to 8.5? No problem. So he kept on jabbing at the pace button, going up past ten miles an hour where he'd never been before. The treadmill underneath him moved so fast he couldn't tell his feet apart, didn't know which arm to swing next. But he didn't fall, and started to feel like he'd never fall, and right then he felt the first pieces of skin pull away from his body like old paint flecking off in the wind.

Dig for Dollars

I F YOU DIDN'T KNOW Andrea you might think she
was just getting love handles, the way a man does when
he gets fat. Growing out sideways in your first trimester, according to some old wives' tale, is supposed to be a sign that
you're carrying one sex or the other. Neither of us could remember which one though.

"Can I listen?" I asked her, putting my ear above her navel,
and she pushed it down a few inches. I closed my eyes and heard
nothing but the ocean crashing in at us, which obliterated any
sound our baby might have made. We were alone on a sandbar
fifty yards from shore, and if the tide held we'd stay right there
until I had to drive her to the airport.

"It doesn't kick yet," Andrea said. In German you call a baby
it—*das Kind,* gender neutral. This is an official part of the language, unlike in English where we call a baby *it* only until we
know better.

"I hear it. It says 'Daddy, daddy!'"

"American baby? I think it's lower." She slid up on the blanket
to get my ear down by her bikini line, and I watched a few grains
of sand fall into her navel. Maybe they'd still be there when her

plane landed back in Munich. Maybe one of them would work its way inside her, and grow in our baby's hand like a pearl. The wind swooped low and plucked Andrea's straw hat off her face, and I jumped up to fetch it from the water. When I handed it back I kissed her the way a man ought to kiss his wife, though Andrea showed no sign whatsoever of wanting to be my wife.

"I'll miss you." She snugged the hat to her head. "I had a great time."

"I'll miss you too. And your little friend." I mock-pinched her belly and she checked her watch.

"We turn over, no?" Andrea was as *punktlich* and *ordentlich* as any stereotypical German you can imagine. Every fifteen minutes exactly we had to flip over, or roll on our sides like rotisserie chickens, to keep from getting too sunburned in any one spot — even though it was only March, and she'd barely see the sun again for months once she got home. She squeezed out sunscreen and rubbed it on my too-pale back. I felt like we were an old married couple, twenty years from now with our kid in college.

"Soon we go to the airport," she said, her hair flopping sideways as she lay on her side. Ten weeks in Florida had made her blond almost to the roots.

"I hope it's a safe flight."

"You know this flight. It's a safe flight."

After that I didn't feel like we were an old married couple anymore. I felt like we were strangers who could barely communicate, who had no business reproducing. In an hour I'd be driving her to the airport and wondering who the hell she really was. Holding her bags while she got her boarding pass, walking her solemnly to the security line. Giving her one last kiss before she put her purse and shoes through the X-ray machine and disappeared until the "someday" we promised to see each other again. She wanted to be pregnant awhile, maybe even have the baby, before she figured out what to do about us.

"We see what happens," she always told me whenever I brought up the future. Which at least was consistent, since we'd never once planned anything. She'd been best friends with Bianca, the German girl I was dating last year, and on Christmas Eve in Munich she told me it was obvious to all their friends that Bianca and I didn't really love each other. Two days later Bianca dumped me on the way to the airport. Four days after that Andrea called to say she'd been laid off and had time to travel, and had always wanted to see America. Could she start her vacation in Tampa? See the ocean? By Martin Luther King Day, she was sleeping in my bed. By Valentine's Day, she was pregnant.

And through all this, nothing surprised her. Andrea never freaked out, never asked herself questions like "What do I really want?" or "Where's my life going?" American questions, she called them. I wanted to surprise her just once, do something that would really drop her jaw. The closest I got was when I asked her to marry me and stay in Tampa, but that got me only wide eyes, a kiss on the cheek, and a sweet laugh. I didn't ask again, though I thought about it hard as we broiled on the sandbar, an hour before she said goodbye.

"I'm getting fat," I told her the next time we turned over.

"It isn't good having no fat." Andrea knew this definitively because she was a nutritional nurse. She spoke about food the way a Prussian general might speak about his troops—efficiency, maximization of benefits, prevention of loss. She had a poor professional opinion of my favorite restaurants, and found me new ones. "Too-skinny people can't fight diseases."

"Thank you, *Doktor Andrea*."

"I would be a very good doctor," she declared, settling down on her belly.

"Isn't that bad for the baby? Laying like that?"

"You worry too much about the baby. I like some here, please."

She patted herself on the small of the back, so I knelt beside her and rubbed the sunscreen on, sliding my hand under her waistband and tickling her tailbone. That's how things started the night I got her pregnant, and I wanted to do it all over again—knowing it this time, planning it.

"Danny, we're in public." Andrea tried to swat my hand away.

"What public? We're fifty yards from anybody."

She clucked her tongue three times and pointed to the other end of the sandbar, where a mother and daughter emerged from the water. The mom had on a blue one-piece racing suit, with thighs as big as a bike racer's bulging out of it. Her daughter was a preschool blur of pink and ponytails. They looked at us briefly, not waving, then kept walking. Probably locals, who knew just how far out you can walk if the tide's right.

"Maybe I am like her one day," Andrea said.

"Don't let your legs get so big. Please."

"I mean maybe I have a daughter like her one day." She turned over on her back even though our fifteen minutes hadn't elapsed. "I wish I could be in Germany now, then I have sun on my breast."

"It's *breasts* in English, two of them."

"*Danke.*" She smacked me a kiss.

"*Bitte.*" I blew one back. "But in Germany you won't have sun until July."

"Ha!" Andrea playfully snarled up her nose at me. I rolled over too, and watched the super-athlete mom walk through the water with her daughter. There was no husband in sight—maybe that's what Andrea meant when she said she'd be like that woman someday. After all, I might not be there the first time she took our baby to the beach, and I could hear them talking in German about why daddy lived so far away. I listened hard to their imaginary conversation, hoping to learn something, but the German got too fast for me. Our baby was a girl at first, like the kid in the water, then a boy. It kept flipping, never settled.

"I'm doing it." Andrea slipped off her bikini top. "It's only one hour. They can arrest me into jail."

This time I didn't correct her English. I resisted the temptation to give myself one last look at her topless torso by pretending I was on a German beach where nobody bothered noticing such things, then by digging my hand underneath me to poke around for sand dollars. Andrea saw me doing it and dug her hand in too, the way I taught her on her first day in America, and when her arm slipped in past her elbow I got a real sick feeling that she was going back to Germany to have an abortion without telling me. That would explain how casual she was about being pregnant. Her arm in the sand turned into the arm of some doctor, reaching inside her and ripping out our baby. Not even looking at it, just throwing it into the garbage. It would end up in a dump or in some filthy river where catfish and eels fought over it and tore it to pieces.

"I've got one." Andrea bit her lower lip.

"Get under it, let it fall into your hand."

She nodded, grunted, and pulled her arm out with a little sand dollar balanced on her palm. It looked beige, not bleached white like the ones you find on the surface, but it was obviously too stiff to be alive. She hopped up and pranced ahead to rinse it off in the ocean.

"A good memory for the baby, no?"

"A Tampa sand dollar for a baby born in Munich. Makes sense, I guess."

"Give it good luck." Andrea kissed the top of my head and put the sand dollar in front of my mouth. I whispered, *Let me know you* under my breath, like the sand dollar was our baby instead. Then I kissed it.

"I hope I'm there to see it born."

"I hope too." Andrea stepped back. "It's a terrible thing if you aren't there."

"So why not marry me and make sure?"

"Because I want to see how you are with the baby. I said this."

"If I'm good with the baby, will you marry me?"

"Yes. I don't think it was a question."

Andrea tucked the sand dollar into her waistband and sat down. She took a few deep breaths to calm herself, though before then I couldn't even tell she'd gotten excited. I didn't know her moods, had no idea how it would feel to live with her. No idea if we'd even be attracted to each other once we had a kid to take care of, or if we lived in Germany instead of America. I didn't know anything about Andrea, really, but I was less scared of marrying her than of being a deadbeat dad. I didn't want to fall in love with some American girl two years down the road and have to tell her about my kid in another country. And if I didn't get to watch Andrea's belly grow, then who knows how much I'd feel like flying over to watch that baby come out? It'd be like somebody else's kid without the whole nine months of watching.

"Why not have it here?" I said. "I have a job, we can —"

"Free hospital, I told you. And my family is there. Here I have only you."

A hundred yards in front of us, the super-athlete woman stood in the ocean up to her chin and perched her daughter on her shoulders. She'd reached the edge of a shelf, and if she took another step they'd both be in over their heads. I'd done that a thousand times, hanging out at the edge on my tiptoes to tempt fate before I headed back to safety. Once in a while a wave knocked the woman back a bit and they both went under, but they always came up whooping. I wanted to do that with my own kid, right there on that same shelf, and I almost gave Andrea an ultimatum: marry me and stay here or I'll never see the baby, never come live with you, never give that kid any pieces of its father except the pictures you already have.

"*Ich hab dich Lieb*," I said instead. I could only tell her I loved her in German.

"*Ich auch.* Please don't ask me to marry you now. I go too soon."

I nodded and looked back at the mother and child in front of us. They bobbed, disappeared in the water, then came up without a whoop this time. Something was different — Andrea and I both sat up. The next time they bobbed, we didn't see them come up.

"Go!" Andrea pushed my shoulder and I raced to where I saw them last. If I saved that woman and her kid, then maybe Andrea would know I'd be okay with our baby and decide to stay. It felt like a test from the universe, to see if I was fit to be a dad, and when the sandbar ended I dove in and started swimming like hell to prove I was. But when I got to where the mother and daughter should have been, I couldn't see anybody. It wasn't a test, I wouldn't pass it, I'd never marry Andrea, I'd never see my baby. I dove past the shelf with my eyes open, flailing around for an arm or leg, until a rip tide started to grab me.

I guess I could have let the rip pull me out to where that woman and her kid were, so I could really try saving them. But there was no use dying for a stranger—especially since I'd have a kid of my own to stay alive for in another eight months—so I chickened out and fought the rip and got back onto the shelf the second I could. *I tried,* is what I'd tell people if that mother and daughter drowned. And I'd be the only one who'd ever have to know I didn't.

Then I saw Andrea halfway down the sandbar, waving and pointing. The mother and daughter were safe fifty yards down-shore, way beyond where I ever could have reached them in time. Either the rip tide dropped them there, or mom's big thighs pulled them through it. She paddled back to shore and didn't look back to let us know they were safe, didn't even acknowledge that I went in after them. Andrea, who glared at the mom looking twice as pissed off as I'd ever seen her, put on her bikini top while I swam back to our spot.

"I tell you. I *never* will do that with our baby."

"Thank you." I fell to my knees, breathing heavy and finally winded from all that swimming. All I wanted to do was find where that baby was in Andrea's belly and kiss her there, as if *das Kind* could kiss me back through her skin. Then she'd know I wasn't afraid to *need* her—that's one word we never used with each other, a word I'd forgotten how to say in German. I had to know it somewhere in my head, it just escaped me. *Hilfen? Haben?* No. But the word wouldn't come, so I just gave Andrea's belly a few little pecks to say goodbye.

At the airport we had a nice last kiss and finally said we loved each other in English. Whenever the conversation petered out one of us would bitch about that woman with the big thighs, and act superior. We'd never be that way with our own kid, we kept saying, like the kid was some kind of theory instead of a living thing in the middle of Andrea. My whole drive home I thought about the German word for *need,* going through the whole alphabet in my head ten times over while I tried to find it. But it still wouldn't come, and I didn't have a German dictionary at home anymore. Didn't have any friends who I could ask, either. So I filed the question away, told myself I'd ask Andrea when she called to say that she'd landed safe, like she promised she would no matter what time of day it was here.

But you can't ask a question like that without going into the whole story, without explaining why you have to know. Without saying *I need you* too soon, the way some people say *I love you* too soon, and maybe screwing up everything.

Bill

MYRA WARE AND I MET as we stumbled through law school together, and by the time we both failed the Massachusetts bar exam for the second time we were engaged and all but living together. We made a great match in so many ways—our sleeping habits, our sex drives, our matching paralegal jobs with rival law firms, our mutual love of Chesapeake Bay retrievers—but we had money issues. More specifically, Myra had issues with the money I spent buying used clothes from Bill Dunlop, a retired doctor in Peterborough, New Hampshire.

Myra had resented my attraction to used clothing and furniture right from the start, and I think it boiled down to the simple fact that my family's money was older than hers. I trusted my own judgment, and knew I'd only buy things with an intrinsic value that time could not diminish. My family has managed to thrive in America for 337 years precisely because of this mentality. We buy quality things, used or not, and refuse to succumb to trendiness the way Myra's parents did—and as she did unconsciously, despite how vehemently she complained about her father's flair for ostentation. Maybe I was supposed to balance her out, like the cash-poor landed gentry in Jane Austen's England used to balance out the nouveau riche merchant families that married into them. Not that my family was cash poor, by any means.

"I like them," she said after our first Christmas dinner together. Eighteen people at my grandfather's house in Arlington, all sitting at one big table with matching place settings. "They have culture without working for it, without having to show it off."

But I don't think Myra ever understood that the "culture" she liked so much was a byproduct of centuries of frugal living. We save our pennies and check every seam on every piece of clothing we buy so that we can pay for what's important. The men in my family don't need two dozen sport coats and three dozen pairs of shoes, like Myra's father. We need six sport coats and six pairs of shoes of sufficient quality to last a lifetime, and perhaps pass on to someone else in the family when the moment is right. Case in point: I own a pair of oxblood Orvis loafers that once belonged to my great uncle Rex. He'd bought them as a fiftieth birthday present to himself and passed them on to me after he stopped walking at eighty-six. They fit me perfectly, and I will never need to purchase another pair of oxblood loafers. If I ever have a son or nephew with the same shoe size, he will not either.

It's the Burchill way. On any given weekend you'll find us at flea markets and garage sales, looking for things other people were too stupid to recognize as potentially valuable. I keep my best finds and sell the rest to my uncle George, who owns an antique shop in Gloucester. Or to my aunt Janet, who owns one in Newton. Or to my great-aunt Isabel, who owns one in Salem and another in Nahant. We consider our ability to spot salvageable junk to be an almost genetic trait — one that would undoubtedly pass on to my offspring whether their mother liked it or not.

Myra had a problem with this. She bought what was fashionable and replaced it when it fell out of style, and viewed my family's hand-me-down habits as déclassé. That's where she was wrong. Though I know some Burchills in the Maine backwoods who hunt squirrels for meat — they're some of my favorites, in fact—the majority of us are presentable, respectable, even emi-nent in our fields. We have doctors, state senators, more lawyers and stockbrokers than anybody can count, an internationally rec-ognized astrophysicist, and a one-time NCAA record-holder in the pole vault. We buy used things, but we are not slouches.

Myra's father—actually a stepfather, which explained more than she wanted to admit—was a hotshot high-tech CEO despite the fact that he couldn't tell *it's* from *its*. He'd come into an un-derperforming company, terrify everyone who he didn't fire into working like a maniac, raise the stock price, and pocket millions when he jumped ship to the next salvage mission. Thanks to him Myra didn't really need to work, and once we got engaged she would have quit her paralegal job in a second if I hadn't set the bar high by keeping mine. I didn't need to work either; I could easily have sold one of the Back Bay town homes my grandmother gave me and lived off it until I was 193 years old. But I didn't, because I place a higher value on work and things that withstand the test of time—whether it's real estate or a vintage silk tie—than I do on my ostensible purchasing power.

"I know it's good quality," Myra said while she watched me strip an 1866 roll-top desk that I bought for $20. Some idiot had painted it orange. "But still, it's stuff other people were going to throw away."

"You know my great-aunt and uncle, up in Bangor?"

"Helga, is that her name?"

"Hannah and Bob. All they do is putter around and collect old stuff, both of them. They're happier than us, saner than us, and they'll live forever."

"Is that what you want from your life? Living long enough to get old?"

"Uh, yeah, I do." It seemed like a stupid question, and the fact that Myra asked it should have told me a lot about her priorities. "Would you trust anybody who *doesn't*?"

Myra stood with her arms crossed and watched the paint bub-ble. One month and two days later, after a year and a half of serious negotiations on marriage, Myra gave me back her ring. Everybody in my family said it was a good thing, which surprised me because they'd always treated her like such a great catch. If she was too snooty to buy secondhand clothes, they said at the dinner table, she'd be a lousy wife and a worse mother. And, they added later in private, lazy in bed in no time.

The crisis point in our relationship came the second weekend in July, when we double-booked ourselves thanks to a miscommunication. I wanted to go to Peterborough for the flea market; Myra wanted to go to Providence for supposedly spectacular Brazilian food, a choral ensemble that performed the works of Benjamin Britten, and shopping at a boutique that sold nothing but hand-crafted lampshades.

Trying to hit both places in one weekend is suicidal given Boston traffic, but Myra and I agreed to try. We'd hit the road at five A.M. Saturday for Providence, then again at five A.M. Sunday for Peterborough. Things were settled. I insisted on driving the whole way because I didn't appreciate the way she drove my 1978 Blazer, which I liked to use for antiquing and which she groused about our whole time in Providence. Not the kind of car one goes boutiquing in, I guess. All that driving made me grouchy once I realized that I'd missed the flea market's opening—that crystalline moment when every single old thing shines like it could be the prize, the find, the gem.

"It'll still be there when we show up," Myra said as I waited to get across a bridge under construction. She melted away the tension in my fists with her fingertips. "That *one thing* you want, it'll be there. Nobody else will even see it."

The woman knew how to calm me down, and I figured that was a great sign for our impending marriage. She'd get used to shopping for antiques and I'd get used to shopping for designer lampshades, or whatever the latest fashion was, and we'd get along fine. We finally got to the flea market and separated awhile, since she liked to amble around browsing and I liked to hunt ferociously for that *one thing* I had to have. Myra was looking through a box of old China, really getting into the spirit, when I spotted a big pile of men's clothes on a table, and more on a blanket below. They were high quality, the kind of stuff my family would happily pass down through the generations. I didn't see the seller immediately, but when I put his clothes to my body they looked like they'd fit. Two minutes later a man came back from behind a white van nearby and stood behind the table. He looked about eighty, but he still had a full head of hair and didn't stoop or lean. He had knobby knuckles from arthritis and long, delicate fingers. Pianist's fingers.

"Name's Bill," he said, giving me a curt, matter-of-fact nod.

"Price." I gave the nod back. He had the same build as me — tall, lanky, a bit long-waisted, shoulders too big for his chest. If his face were anything like mine, I would have felt like I was staring at myself fifty years older. I got so spooked that I couldn't look at him, and took an armful of clothes into his van to try them on. I came out three minutes later wearing Bill's blue jeans, Bill's tan chamois shirt, and Bill's red windbreaker. They all fit me perfectly.

"You're sure we're not related?" I asked him.

"Don't know. What's your last name?"

"Burchill. Family's from Salem originally."

"Got any Dunlops in with 'em? I'm a Dunlop."

"None I've met. Whelans, Parkers, Hendrys, Grants."

"Nope, don't have any of those. How about Adam and Eve, you know them?"

We laughed and shook hands, and over Bill's shoulder I noticed Myra walking toward us with her head cocked like she was seeing double. Bill and I both had the same rooted way of standing, the same way of leaning in close when we talked. In her shoes, I wouldn't have minded the resemblance — if I can stand up as straight as Bill Dunlop when I'm eighty, I'll be mighty happy. But Myra's eyes narrowed fast when she saw Bill's clothes on my body, and I broke the handshake.

"G'morning." Bill gave her that same curt nod.

"This is my fiancée, Myra Ware." I put a hand on Bill's shoulder and turned him around. He looked Myra up and down in a flash.

"I think my wife's got some clothes that'll fit you," Bill said, and a wrinkle of disgust rippled across Myra's nose.

"Oh please." She placed her hand ever-so-sweetly over her heart. "I've already got more clothes than I know what to do with."

"So do I. Doesn't stop me." I did a silly pirouette to show how comfortable I felt in Bill's clothes. "These feel like I was born in them."

"Well they're almost old enough so you could've been," she mumbled.

I winked at Myra and knelt down to paw through the rest of Bill's clothes. If I had to stand around pretending to care about lampshades made of alpaca, then she had to pretend to care about the seams on a fifty-year-old jacket. Period. I tried to hand her the clothes I'd worn on the trip up, but Myra didn't feel like holding them and I put them on the bare ground instead. She looked at me like she was throwing all her previous impressions of me out the window and replacing them with new, less flattering ones. Future husband on hands and knees scrounging through an old man's castoff clothes. Future husband more interested in old junk than in Benjamin Britten and gourmet Brazilian food. I didn't feel like acknowledging Myra's vibe, so I talked to Bill instead.

"I bet this one's got a story." I held up a black corduroy vest that Myra would have loved if only she didn't hate the idea of me touching it.

"They've all got stories. That's from my brother's wedding, 1959. I've got more like that, dress stuff. Most of this is for around the house."

"I'd like to see those sometime."

"I'm here every other Sunday. Get in early and we'll have coffee."

"I'll do that." I nodded emphatically, sealing my commitment just loud enough so Myra couldn't pretend she never heard it.

"Good. What do you do?"

"We're in law school." I looked at Myra and we both felt the lie, which we'd agreed upon for strangers. We were officially done with school, but since we hadn't passed the bar exam we called ourselves students to cut down on the explanation.

"I used to be a doctor." Bill looked at the ground, so suddenly aimless that I wondered if I'd said something wrong.

"Are you selling your little black bag?" Myra asked him, and for a moment Bill and I both pretended she was a real sport. The laugh we all shared acted as a segue to the next phase of my flea market purchase experience: the excruciating decision of what to take and what to leave. Myra always hurried me through this, and it drove me nuts. Left to my own devices, I literally would have tried on every piece of clothing I liked until I found the right three or four. I think Bill would have been proud to see me get that meticulous about his old stuff, and he was probably disappointed when I caved in to Myra's scornful gaze and started grabbing things indiscriminately.

I lost control, I admit it. I gave Bill $100 and asked him to pile clothes on my arms until we had a fair deal. By the time he stopped, Myra and I both had such huge piles to carry that we couldn't even wave goodbye to him, or see our feet on the way to the Blazer. We walked gingerly all the way back, hoping those soft clothes would cushion the fall if we tripped. People got out of our way and looked admiringly at us, saying things that made Myra bristle — "Nice haul!" and "You'll never have to buy clothes again!"

"Shit," I muttered as I opened my tailgate. "I left my old clothes."

"What are you talking about?"

"My old clothes, the ones I came up here with."

"They aren't old, Price. They're almost brand-new."

"You know what I mean. I've got to go back."

"No," she said. "If you go back, you'll buy everything he owns. *I'm* going."

"You don't have—"

"I'm *going,* sweetie."

While Myra walked to the flea market and back, I went through all of Bill's clothes and arranged them on the back seat according to type and condition. There were a few clunkers—like a blue Norwegian sweater with holes in both elbows—but for the most part I'd scooped up unbelievable bargains. Two Irish cable-knit sweaters that would have cost $120 each new. Three pairs of wool trousers. Flannel shirts without a single fray on the collar or the sleeves. Long johns. Thick hiking socks. A fur-lined leather hat.

"This stuff smells," Myra said when she got back to the Blazer. "I can't tell if it's mold or mothballs. Fungus, something."

"So I'll dry clean it." I wanted to show her the craftsmanship on a pair of blue chinos, but knew she'd only see their age. "How often do you run into somebody who's got *exactly* the same body as you, and he's practically giving away all his clothes? And they're all broken in, you should feel them."

"They're not broken in, they're *worn out.* They'll all end up in plastic bags in your garage. You won't wear them."

"That's not true."

"Okay, you'll wear them for a couple days, until you realize they're caked with dust, and *then* they'll end up in plastic bags in your garage. If you want different clothes, I'll go shopping with you. I'll buy it for you, so you don't have to spend anything."

"It's not about spending money."

"I know, it's about you pretending that clothes have more meaning just because somebody else wore them before you. But they *don't.*" She hung her head and snorted. "Every time this happens I tell myself I can't live this way. I can't be married to a pack-rat."

I hadn't heard that word in at least three months. Myra said *packrat* only in her most vicious, angry moments of rebellion against my buying habits, though I suspect she thought it all the time. I shut the back door as gently as possible.

"Why? Worried our kids'll have fuzzy tails and whiskers, steal all your buttons?"

"It's not funny, Price. There's something sick about it, like you're trying to be somebody else. Can we go home now, please?" She got in the passenger seat. As I sat behind the wheel she wiped the dust from Bill's clothes off her hands and put the stuff I'd worn on the way up between her feet.

"Don't you want some lunch?"

"No, let's just go home. Price—?" She turned and put her hand on my forearm, the way she did when she really wanted me to listen. But then she realized she was touching Bill's chamois shirt and pulled away. "Just the idea of sleeping next to you after you wear all those old clothes—I get the creeps. It's not some abstract, metaphysical thing, it physically makes my flesh crawl. I want you to be *you*."

"I *am* me. And I want you to be you, too." I started up, revving the engine like it hadn't run in weeks. "Is that it?"

"That's it." Myra dusted her hands again and folded them in her lap, then sat in silence. I kept my mouth shut even though I had plenty more to say—most of all that she'd better get that nouveau riche stick out of her ass before we got married. Where did she get off talking to me about *being myself* when her whole personality, her twist-in-the-wind fashions, her stupid alpaca lampshade, existed simply to cover up the fact that she used to eat ketchup on Wonder Bread for dinner until she finally got herself a dad at age six?

As soon as I got going fast enough to calm down, a dilapidated Ford wagon sputtered onto the road in front of me without even looking. Myra screamed and practically hit the windshield when I braked, and I gave it a long, yowling honk. The Ford, farting blue smoke all over the two-lane, honked right back and swerved in front of me whenever I tried to pass it. I finally got by on the right shoulder, fishtailing a little. There were three white college kids inside, looking stoned as hell, and I gave them my middle finger eight or ten times. Then one of the kids threw a can of soda at my Blazer—sure, it's a shitbox, but it's *my* shitbox—and hit the

back window. I zipped ahead and stopped, then grabbed the claw
hammer I keep under my seat just in case I need to open my mal-
functioning hood. I didn't even look at Myra as I got out.

"Price, what are you doing?" She locked her door and crouched
down in her seat.

"Teaching some pricks a lesson." The wagon rolled up and
stopped, and the college kids came out swearing. I had the hammer behind my back, and swung it in their faces once they came
within striking distance. The kids got pale real fast, like they just
remembered they were too stoned to scare anybody, and hurried
back to the Ford.

"Not so tough now, huh?" I yelled. "Yeah, go back to your
mommies."

The whole episode resembled absolutely nothing in my personal history. Maybe Myra was right, and I'd started to turn into
somebody else from buying too many old clothes. It's nothing Bill
Dunlop would have done, though the squirrel-eating Burchills up
in Maine would have pulled out their shotguns right away.

"What if they had a gun?" Myra said when I climbed in. "We
could've died."

"White college stoners don't carry guns, honey." I put the
hammer back under my seat and tried starting the engine even
though it was still running. Its sharp grind made me jump worse
than those kids did when they felt my hammer in their faces. "I'm
hungry and I want some food. We're stopping for food at the next
place we see."

On Tuesday night I took Myra out for a $300 dinner, apologized
for the hammer incident, and blamed my poor behavior on a
free-floating malaise caused by my failure to pass the bar. Myra
bought it, and even commiserated. We called in sick and spent
the next two days sequestered in the bedroom of her North End
condo, safely distanced from my most recent secondhand ac-
quisitions. We considered going to one of the couples counsel-
ors we'd researched, but never actually called for an appointment.
The next day I put Bill's clothes in my garage where Myra had no

chance to snipe about them. We swept our issues under the rug and moved on.

Things rolled merrily along until the second Friday in August, during which Myra and I fought so hard you'd think we were already married. I wanted to go back up to Peterborough that Sunday and see Bill again, since he'd promised me a look at his dress clothes, while Myra wanted to go to New York on the spur of the moment.

"You didn't even like New York last time," I reminded her as we nibbled away at sushi that I could have made myself for half the price. "You said it smelled disgusting."

"No, I said the bum on the subway smelled disgusting. Take away the bum and it was a great trip."

"You complained about the dim sum, I remember. But you complain about your food all the time."

"What's that supposed to mean?"

"Face it, you just don't want to go to Peterborough again. You're scared of Bill. Or of his clothes, at least."

"Absolutely untrue." Myra got all imperious on me, lifting her chin in the air and only looking at me askance, then launched into a lecture about why I shouldn't want to buy Bill Dunlop's clothes. Or anyone else's, for that matter. Or even antique furniture.

1) Because none of the things I ever bought used were worth the time I spent fixing them, or even poking at them to determine their value.

2) Because every time I found something of halfway decent quality, I practically gave it away to some aunt or uncle and let them make all the profit, while I barely covered the cost of gasoline to cart it around from its original home to their store.

3) Because there's a difference between having class and taste and simply wanting to fill your life with old junk, no matter how much you respect the quality of the junk or the people who used to own the junk.

4) Because I'd spend more money to dry clean Bill's clothes than I'd spent to purchase them.

5) Because I had to buy some *new* clothes every once in a
   while to keep from looking like I'd been cryogenically
   frozen for fifty years.
6) Because it's just plain creepy to own so much old clothing
   that belonged to somebody who wasn't even in your
   family, and who smells like he's getting ready to die.

The word *packrat* did not leave Myra's mouth once. As an
emotional appeal, her speech was not without merit. As a well-
reasoned argument—well, let's say the wannabe-lawyer in me
could have taken it down with marbles in his mouth.

"Are you finished?" I asked her. She nodded, too spent to say
yes or no. I responded by pulling out my wallet and making two
piles of cash.

"This is for your trip to New York," I said of the larger pile,
"and this is for dinner tonight. I'm going home, I'm getting some
sleep, and I'm going antiquing this weekend."

Myra looked around the restaurant as if for reinforcements.
When no one looked our way, she lowered her head and whispered, "Why are you doing this?"

"Same reason you gave me the packrat speech, hon. It's called
communication."

"Don't get condescending with me."

"I'm not getting condescending with you. I'm simply telling
you the truth of who I am. You either accept that truth, or we
have no future."

I stood up, kissed her neck, and left. An hour later Myra
showed up at my place, said I was right, and vowed to accept who
I was. We talked until two in the morning, going around and
around on the same old things, and she slept on my couch even
though we'd made up ten times over.

Then we compromised on the weekend. Mostly, *I* compromised.
We spent Saturday cleaning my garage and attempting to arrive at
some mutual sense of how to distinguish a valuable or charming

antique from worthless junk. I took two full truckloads to the Salvation Army, and upon my return I caught Myra digging through the big plastic bag that contained the clothes I'd purchased from Bill. Wisely, she closed the bag without a word. I cooked that night—linguine with clam sauce that completely outstripped the overpriced version at Myra's favorite Italian place—and we left at five A.M. Sunday morning so I could catch Bill Dunlop for that cup of coffee he promised.

"Do you think we'll run into that old station wagon?" Myra asked on the way up, trying valiantly to turn last month's nightmare into an engagement-saving joke. We talked about where and when to get married, where we wanted to buy a house, and whether to keep our condos. It seemed like we were on track again.

Then we got to the flea market in time to watch Bill set up a card table and lay out not more men's clothes, but *women's* clothes. Multicolored polyester dresses from the sixties and seventies, sweaters Myra would swim in, fur-lined winter coats, pink leather gloves. Bill laid the clothes out gingerly, didn't see me and Myra coming, and went back to his van for another load. A pile of suits beckoned me from a blanket on the ground and I got on my knees to look through it.

"These must be his doctor suits," I told Myra, and when I glanced up she was bristling at the women's clothes. Bill came back from his van with a big smile for her—which surprised me, since he didn't seem to like her much the first time they met.

"I brought some of my wife's stuff." Bill set down his next armload, which featured a mauve sequined dress and a pea green linen jacket. Myra politely felt the jacket, avoided touching the dress, and watched Bill go back to the van again.

"I hope he doesn't expect me to buy these," she whispered to me. "I already told him I had more clothes than I knew what to do with."

"Try something on, at least. Humor him."

"That's *your* thing, not mine."

Bill's next load had only a single item: a white waistcoat of finer quality than any piece of clothing Myra owned, though she would never admit that. It was obviously a semi-sacred relic to him, and I hushed in involuntary reverence to it.

"Try this on," Bill said. "It's half wool, half cashmere. Anniversary present."

"No," Myra waved it off. "She should keep that. It's too—"

"She's confined to bed, miss. Somebody ought to wear it."

Myra smiled at Bill, though not at me, and tried on the coat. From the look on her face it must have smelled hideous to her, but she was a trooper and kept it on for a while. Even turned around and modeled it for me.

"It's a hell of a coat," I told her, and Bill nodded in agreement. But I could tell Myra felt old and conservative in it, and somewhat ghoulish because it belonged to a woman who couldn't even get out of bed.

"It feels like cashmere," Myra declared. "A little big in the shoulders, though."

"Otherwise it fits her pretty well, I think." Bill said, more to me than to Myra.

"It does." I held her hand a moment. "Try something else on if this doesn't fit."

"I think this'd look pretty." Bill handed her the awful mauve sequined dress. "You're almost her size. Can't hurt." He went back to his van for more.

"You creep," Myra hissed at me. The white coat came off in a flash. "You're going to make me walk away from here with everything she ever wore."

"I'm asking you to do a favor for an old man whose wife is dying, that's all."

"Who says she's dying?"

"When people can't leave their beds, they're dying. Just try on the dress. I'll buy it and give it to one of my aunts. You'll never see it again."

"Only because I love you," Myra seethed through clenched teeth, just loud enough for Bill to hear. He waved her over to his van and she huffed toward it with the dress, her shoulders pulled violently back. Bill smiled at me like nothing was wrong, and in a way, nothing was. In a way, Myra and I were bit players in a much grander drama about Bill Dunlop and his dying wife. And I could accept that—I had the humility to know that sometimes you walk into somebody else's play for a minute, say your lines as passionately as possible, and leave. You try on a dress that somebody else used to love wearing. You give an old man with a dying wife a little smile before they're both done smiling forever.

"She'll look pretty in it," Bill assured me as I squatted by his card table, earmarking the suits I wanted.

"Was it another anniversary present?"

"Tenth. She was your wife's age, maybe a bit older."

"Myra's my fiancée."

"Well your fiancée's age, then."

Bill and I went back about our business because we didn't want to talk about Myra. We both knew the play we were acting in, like we'd read it in high school and again in college. I knew he needed to see a beautiful young woman in his wife's tenth anniversary dress. He knew I'd help him because I understood tradition and respect for my elders, and I guess he assumed that Myra understood them too. But she hadn't grown up with that play, and needed things like tradition and respect spelled out for her. Deep in my heart, I know that the woman I'm meant to marry doesn't need to have them explained. She'd take that mauve dress home and get it sized just right. She'd let me take pictures of her in it and I'd bring them back to Bill, so he could show his wife that he still remembered how beautiful she used to look.

Goddamnit, that's the woman I want.

Instead I had Myra Ware, who came out of Bill's van looking miserable. She curled her lip in protest against the dress, which didn't fit and made her skin look green. Bill didn't see how horribly the dress fit, he saw how his wife looked on their tenth anniversary. And you know what? So did I. He held his hands out in front of him like he was waiting for Myra to step into a kiss.

"What's your wife's name?" I asked him.

"Ann."

"It doesn't really fit." Myra sneezed three times.

"It needs a little work," I told her. "We can fix it up."

"I don't sew, and neither do you." Myra simpered demonically, saving her rage for when she got me alone, then headed back to Bill's van. When she came out, she marched straight for the parking lot and didn't look back at me. Bill retrieved the mauve dress from his van and put it back on the pile. I hastily picked out my favorite half-dozen suits and reached for my wallet.

"How much for the dress?" I asked him. "And the coat?"

"Nothing. On the house."

"No, it's a nice dress. That coat's cashmere."

"On the house." He squeezed my shoulder. "Doctor's orders."

I handed Bill three fifties for the suits, and he didn't try to give me change. I folded them over my arm and he laid the coat and dress on top of them. His hand lingered on the dress awhile, maybe remembering how his wife's hip used to feel under it.

"Are you sure you want us to have these?" I almost added *since we're probably breaking up tonight.*

"Sure. You'll find them a good home." Maybe Bill could tell I had aunts who'd love the stuff. I'm sure he could tell that Myra and I were doomed.

"Next month?"

"You bet. I'll pull some winter stuff out."

I shook his hand and ambled back to the parking lot, stopping to look at a mahogany bed frame somebody wanted only $200 for. Why hurry? I checked out a little cabinet made of pressed tin that looked like it came from out west somewhere, instead of New England, but I didn't feel confident that any of my relatives would like it. So I walked back to the Blazer and found Myra behind the wheel; she gunned the engine and hovered on the edge of first gear while I neatly stacked my new suits on the back seat.

"Put that junk in back, please." It wasn't a request, but an order. And I didn't mind taking orders from her right then, since I knew we'd never make love again. I put the suits in the cargo

space with the crumpled mauve dress and white coat, and three
minutes later our breakup was permanent and official.

Ten days after that Ann Dunlop died in Bill's arms, but from
what I heard you couldn't exactly call it a romantic scene. Ann
started spitting up blood, along with some putrid yellow bile, and
five minutes later the spirit left her in a flash. She had so many
things wrong with her that Bill, despite his decades of doctoring,
didn't even try to guess her cause of death. He let everything she'd
spewed up sit right there on the bedroom floor, where it caked up
and hardened.

   Bill dragged her body out onto the front lawn and started
digging a grave for her, and refused to be stopped by the kindly
neighbors and town authorities who came by to dispose of her
body more properly. One of the men who tried to stop him took
a shovel in the neck, and got tetanus shots for his trouble. The
cops finally hauled Bill down and took him to a state mental hospital thirty miles away. He stayed seventy-two hours for observation, talked to the brother-in-law who was his only surviving
family, and then seemed well enough to go home. Ann was buried at a church cemetery, and Bill watched without incident. He
gave boxes and boxes of her things to Goodwill and the Salvation
Army. He slept during the day and stayed up all night, as Ann had
done for the last three months of her life—it seemed to be the
one thing she'd left him that anybody could tell.

   I didn't find this out from Bill directly, but from another ven-
dor at the Peterborough flea market when I went up there, as a
newly single man, in September. I wore the blue jeans, chamois
shirt, and red windbreaker I'd bought from Bill the first time we'd
met, hoping they would signal that I'd ditched the snooty fiancée
who didn't like old clothes. I felt like an idiot wearing them when I
couldn't find him, like an impostor. It took half an hour of asking
questions to get anybody to admit they even knew him—though
the look in their eyes said otherwise—and another hour before
his neighbor Brett filled me in.

"It surprised a lot of people how he got in the end," Brett told me. "If you're older than five or six and born here, chances are fifty-fifty he delivered you. He delivered me."

"Were you with him that night?"

"I was there on the lawn, sure. Wasn't the same Bill, though. If you're thinking about seeing him, you should think twice."

I tried unsuccessfully to wheedle Bill's address from Brett, but did pick up the name of their street: Parmenter Road. A few gas station conversations later I was there, checking out the front lawn of every house I passed. On my second try I saw a big scar on the lawn of 1217 — there was no new sod over it, no seed, nothing. I wondered if I could ever love a woman enough to go crazy for her and try burying her in our front yard, but couldn't imagine mustering that feeling for anybody. Maybe you have to be married fifty years before you can go that crazy, I don't know.

But I'd have to ask myself that question the next time I started dating somebody, I thought as I knocked on Bill's door. Project myself fifty years into the future and imagine digging her grave, imagine stabbing another man in the neck with a shovel for trying to stop me. If the image fit, then maybe I was meant to marry her. If not, then why waste my time? Such was my pathetic attempt to think like, and not merely dress like, Bill Dunlop.

Nobody answered the door, though after my second knock it swung open on its hinges. I found Bill asleep on a blue couch, which was the only piece of furniture left in his living room. He'd stacked boxes everywhere, all carefully numbered. I knocked on a wall and shuffled my feet to wake Bill up. He didn't look crazy and seemed to recognize me right away.

"Sorry to hear about your wife," I told him.

"It happens. How's yours?"

"She wasn't my wife yet. Won't be, either."

"Good." Bill tried to roll himself up from the couch but fell back into it, so I gave him a hand. He looked at his old clothes on me the way you look at somebody you know but whose name you've forgotten, then started marching slowly and unsteadily across the living room. "Got to show you something," he mumbled, all business as he led me into his office, the walls of which were lined with beautiful and completely empty cherrywood bookshelves. In the middle of the room sat a black desk and matching leather chair, which Bill plopped down into. He reached for a binder on the desk, rifled through its pages, and turned it around to me. On the very last sheet of off-white parchment he'd written, in big capital letters:

TO WHOM IT MAY CONCERN

I REALIZE THAT SINCE MY WIFE'S DEATH, MY
BEHAVIOR HAS NOT BEEN ENTIRELY RATIONAL.
HOWEVER I HOPE YOU WILL ACCEPT THAT I AM
OF SOUND MIND AND BODY WHEN I BEQUEATH
MY CLOTHES AND ACCESSORIES (TIE TACKS,
CUFFLINKS, SHOES, BELTS, HATS, ETC., IN BOXES
#12–16) TO

It ended right there. I leaned over the desk to get at Bill's eye level, but he wouldn't look at me.

"I didn't remember your name," he said. "Didn't know where you were from. I was waiting for you, kept the same pen out and everything."

"Price Burchill," I told him. "Thirty-eight Brewster Street, Cambridge, Mass, 02138. Do you want a card?"

"No, this'll be fine. There won't be too much stuff left, you understand."

"Sure, I already bought most of it." I tugged at the sleeve of his old chamois shirt and forced a laugh, but Bill didn't smile. He slowly wrote my name and address with an old fountain pen, mumbling them repeatedly until he got the last number of my zip code down. Then he capped his pen and blew on the ink. He glanced up at me and I smiled at him, which I guess was a mistake because he turned away and flipped the binder shut.

For a second I got pissed off at him. I'd broken up with the woman I deserved most in the world over some half-alive phantom who barely treated me like a human being—traded a fiancée for a few boxes of old clothes. I almost jumped up and drove straight to Myra's place to beg her forgiveness, tell her that I'd just severed my emotional ties to Bill Dunlop and his junky old clothes. But I couldn't muster up enough passion to grovel, especially in front of her.

"There's one more suit I want to give you." Bill rifled through his drawers until he found a bundle wrapped in tissue paper and tied with gold ribbon. "For now. My best one."

He put it on his desk and immediately looked away. I pulled back the tissue to see the suit: heavy black wool with fine, barely perceptible gold flecks woven deep into the fabric. A doctorly suit, confident and distinguished. If I were a country doctor who delivered half the people in my town, I'd want to be buried in one just like it.

"All my phone numbers are on this." I handed Bill my card after all. "Call me when you need it back."

"Will do." Bill wrote the word *suit* on my card, then set it on his binder.

"Should I try it on?" I asked, remembering how he wanted Myra to try on Ann's dress before she died. "Would you like that?"

"No." Bill put his hand on the suit and held my eyes for the first time since I came over. He looked like he was staring at a wall. "Keep it wrapped, until I need it."

"I'll do that." As Bill moved his hand away, I wondered if I should even bother taking the thing home—maybe I should leave it with the local funeral home, so they could get him into it right away. But he said he wanted me to have the suit, so it would be mine until somebody called me and said he needed it back.

"You should go now." Bill pushed the suit closer to me. "I'm not who I used to be. You can take your boxes now too, if you want. Everybody else is."

"Sure." But I wasn't taking the boxes, now or ever. I stood up

BILL   117

and tucked the suit under my arm. Maybe he had a bit part in my drama, like I had one in his. He ran onstage, shouted, *Don't marry that woman, whatever you do,* then stumbled off and started dying. "I appreciate what you did for me."

"Nothing to appreciate." He swiveled his chair and stared out the window.

"There is. You showed me who I was and who I wasn't."

"Anybody could do that."

"You mean something to me, Dr. Dunlop. And I appreciate what you mean."

"Call me Bill. Like it or not, you always mean something to somebody."

They were the last words I heard him speak. Shit, I thought, walking back to my Blazer with the suit he'd wear forever. They could be the last words anybody hears him speak.

Three A.M.
Ambulance Driver

WE MET AT AN ALL-NIGHT burrito shop in North Hollywood, right near the 101, that's owned and run by a Vietnamese refugee. His name's Chau, and I've bought food from him enough times to justify waving at him whenever I meet him on the street. Except I never do. The woman was sitting two stools down from me at the counter — at the bar, really, because that's what the burrito shop used to be — and we wouldn't have said a word to each other if Chau hadn't mixed up our orders. We would have stared at our newspapers or at our plates and chowed down in silence as if on opposite sides of the universe, both eating a ceremonial last meal.

But Chau gave her the fish and me the chicken, so the woman and I had to lift our heads and look at each other. Not a bad first look. The kind that says, *I recognize you as a fellow human being,* instead of, *Stop staring at me, creep.* She wore a light blue uniform that looked vaguely coplike, and I thought she might be a security guard even though I didn't see a gun at her waist. Would it have been any different if she had one? I pegged her for thirty-nine—she had the slightly wrinkling skin around the corners of her eyes and mouth that women start getting then, when age becomes more insistent about nudging youth off of center stage. She had wavy red hair, probably dyed if its rusty sheen was any indication, that didn't go at all with the blue uniform. Overdone, probably on a whim. Maybe even a desperate, last-chance whim. Green eyes that didn't go with either the hair or the uniform. No ring on her finger, which surprised me because she had a married vibe to her. A settled, *I am who I am and who the hell else cares because it's just me and my family against the world, damnit* kind of vibe. Maybe she couldn't wear the ring to work—company rules. Maybe she was divorced, had two fatherless latchkey kids asleep at home, and needed two jobs to feed them. In that case, thirty-nine was a good age to get married again.

The woman checked out my left hand to see if I had a ring on, just like I did to her. Nothing there, so another smile. The first steps in the copulation waltz of the divorced and depressed, one of America's favorite dances. Each try can lead to the fandango of remarriage, after all. So why not lose yourself in it, go whole hog? Let yourself slide off into the beat? I smiled back, letting my eyes sparkle.

"This one's yours," she told me, eating the bit of my fish burrito that she'd sliced off and keeping the fork that had touched her lips. Then she slid the plate over. I followed her lead and did exactly the same.

"Thanks. No better place to eat at three A.M., huh?"

"Mmm." She sliced off a first bite of her rightful burrito and slugged it down like it was an oyster. She looked ready to eat the whole thing without taking another breath, if she could. Like she hadn't eaten for a day and a half. I cut a dainty bite of mine and chewed dispassionately, if for no other reason than to balance out her fervor.

"I haven't seen you here before," I went on. I was already in a conversation with her, like it or not, and I've found that it's much easier to let conversations go until they reach their natural conclusions than it is to back out of them once they get started. Backing out leaves that interrupted, *Oh, what might have been* kind of feeling behind, and it hangs around in your mouth all day. Diverts you from the present.

"Yes you have," she told me after she swallowed. Then she jerked her thumb behind her, out the window at a waiting ambulance. "That's my rig. You remember that, don't you?"

I turned around and recognized it immediately. Remembered reading the big, red, backwards ECNALUBMA on its front more than once, and thinking of the words you can make out of it. There aren't all that many for a source word so big. *Clan. Clam. Club. Bum. Blame. Able. Amble. Male. Mace.*

"You may not've noticed me," the woman said, "but you've seen me. I've seen you. I just try to stay inobstrusive."

I liked that she tried to use big words, even if she messed them up. "Don't ambulance crews usually have more people?"

"They do, but the guys have another place they like. Across the street and down a block, sort of Thai/Chinese."

"Right, I've eaten there. A Mexican guy runs it." I jerked my chin toward Chau in the kitchen. "Like these guys traded lives."

"Right, the Mexican guy. Here's to America." The ambulance driver laughed and raised her fork like she was making a toast, but didn't try to keep the conversation going after that. She put her head down and ate like I didn't exist, and that only made me study her more. I tried to remember seeing her before, even half a glimpse on the way in or out the burrito shop door, but nothing about her had stuck in my head. Like she said, "unobtrusive." Maybe I'd seen her a hundred times with some other color hair, some boring mousy brown, and hadn't noticed her until she made the change. And just in case that's how things were, I wanted her to know that the dye job was working.

"How does your crew find you when there's a call?" I asked.

"Well, we've got the walkie-talkies." She patted the one on her hip, near where I'd looked for a gun when I thought she was a security guard. "If there's a call we all hear it, and I swing by. I'm more of a—I like to eat alone, usually."

She half-smiled at me, which amounted to her jutting out her lower lip and curling it up a quarter-inch. It's as if the word *loner,* the one she didn't want to say, had stapled itself to her tongue.

"What do *you* do that brings you here at three A.M.?" she asked me, starting to eat more slowly and settle into the counter.

"I train people to emote," I told her as nonchalantly as I could, looking away. That's the only way I can tell people about what I do—out of the corner of my mouth, like it was so typical they'd already met twenty people that day who did it. Like saying I'm in sales, or in software. Something people don't have to add up.

"To *emote?*" She leaned back and craned her neck to look at me sideways. "You a shrink or something?"

"No, more like a motivational speaker. It's hard to explain."

"I'll bet." She took another mouthful of food, chewed it for a few seconds, and swallowed. Then she let out one of those little happy food grunts and put her knife and fork down. Satisfied. The stress of her latest life-saving adventure gone, buried beneath beans and rice and salsa and sour cream. She softened up, drank a sip of water. Then a gulp. Then another. "How can you train people to emote when—I'm sorry for saying this, but you don't come across like a very emotional person. If you don't mind me saying it. I mean, I've seen you here before, and you're always alone. You pay and tip, you say bye to Chau, and you're gone."

"I'm trying to be inobstrusive too. It helps you watch the world."

"That's for damn sure. But how *do* you? Train people to emote when you're . . . ?" She didn't finish the sentence, maybe because the words didn't come and maybe out of politeness. I swear I saw a hint of gray in her roots, a spot she forgot to dye. But it could've been the light, too. I watched that halo of light float down onto her from the ceiling, throwing her shadow onto the bar below her, and thought, *She could be the one. I could make her the one. I could make a thousand women like her the one.*

"When I don't seem very emotional? It's simple. I live a lie. I stand in front of them and I teach them how to emote better than I do. Like I wish I could. Like I can on good days."

"What do you say? Do you sit there and tell him how good it feels, or . . . ?"

"No, I stand up there in front of the room and get their blood pumping. Get their emotions going, in case they forgot they had them. Or buried them."

I stood up and swung my arm in a cheerleaderish, go-get-'em kind of motion. Then I stabbed my index finger through the air at an imaginary audience and got ready to pitch up my voice, to give it plenty of vibrato. I puffed myself up into full-on motivational speaker mode, with a presence big enough for a room of fifty even though there was nobody there but me and the woman.

"You might think the world wants you to bottle up your emotions, but it doesn't! You might think your friends and family want that, but they don't! Because if you don't emote, *everything* builds up inside you. All the things you *wanted* to do, but *stopped* yourself from doing. All your hopes. Everything you *wished* you could be, but wouldn't *let* yourself be, is going to rot inside you and build up, until it explodes or turns into cancer!"

Chau hurried out from the kitchen, looked at me, and retreated. I tried to catch his eye, but he just squinted at something past me. I brushed off my sleeves, slouched back down to normal, and plopped onto my stool.

"Impressive." The woman bunched up her lips, listening now. Definitely listening. "Who do you give these speeches to? These presentations, whatever?"

"Businesses, mostly. Church groups. Schools sometimes."

"To kids?" She pulled her head away from me. It looked like a pigeon bobbing its head, but in reverse.

"To teachers, mostly. But yeah, kids sometimes."

"How old are they?"

"Junior high, I guess. When they start having trouble opening up to their parents. But I've done fourth grade too, a couple times."

"Hmm." She chewed more slowly than I'd ever seen her, and narrowed the one eye I could see. "It's very impressive. And I think it's true, what you said about cancer and heart disease. That's what you meant by 'blowing up,' right?"

"Sure. It fits."

"I see lots of sick people, and it's half and half. They either blow up, or they shrivel up."

"When I see sick people, I want to make them feel better. Don't you?" I realized, as the words dissolved into the air around me, that my voice hadn't quite pulled back from motivational speaker mode even though my body had. So I brought it back inside me. Coaxed it in like a big, dumb fish you can't rush.

"I guess." She shrugged. "I want to *drive* them to people who can make them feel better, at least. I'm not a doctor or anything."

"But you don't *have* to be a doctor to heal people. Just by being human, we're given this healing power that we can share with anybody. It doesn't have to be open-heart surgery. We can heal with light, with sound. With touch."

"Well in my business, you have to be a doctor." And that, to the ambulance driver, was that. She smiled and went back to her burrito, but I couldn't cut the conversation off so fast. To not even *try* getting her to see life the way I saw it, to feel the healing power that's *everywhere* if you open yourself to the world—I wouldn't be able to live with myself. I had to try getting her to see it, even if she didn't understand it right away. Even if it took weeks, months. Even if I never saw her again.

"I'm talking about in everyday *life*," I said, and Chau popped his head out from behind his pans again for a second. "When you see a sick person, doesn't it make you want to hold your hands up to them and pull the sickness right out?"

"No." She clamped her lips together. "Because I can't do that."

"But you *can*. You can pull out everything they didn't let themselves be, so it won't make them sick anymore. No blowing up, no shriveling."

I leaned toward her so quickly that she didn't have time to react, and held my fingertips an inch away from her temples. They hovered there, vibrating, not hurting anybody. It was invasive, sure. But she looked at me like she knew karate or jiu-jitsu and would kick my ass if I got a millimeter closer, or stayed near her a second too long. I nodded at her and leaned back.

"Look at my hands," the ambulance driver said, shoving her palms at my face. They were small, chubby, dry-looking hands with calluses all over them — so many calluses that all the lotion in the world couldn't smooth them out. I could see every whorl of her fingertips, all the creases that nicked at her lifeline and her loveline. See the place where a wedding ring used to live, or might live. A kitchen fan turned off and suddenly there wasn't a sound in the place. Just the woman's hands and me.

"Look at them," she said again, pushing them almost into my eyes. "Do you think I can do that with hands like this? Tell me."

Knuckles

NINETEEN MONTHS AGO I saw my neighbor Lisbeth Pomeroy standing by my curb in perfect mourning. I knew her by sight but had never spoken with her, even though our daily walks took us past the same shrubs and park benches in Boston's Public Garden, from which we both lived a stone's throw away. I'd seen her that day from my second-floor office window: waiting on the sidewalk as magnificently alone as Antigone in her black dress, black veil, black gloves, black purse. A magnificent woman is magnificent all the time, whether she's dressed for the opera or out grilling burgers on the fire escape in a grimy T-shirt. Lisbeth Pomeroy had looked magnificent walking her dog on Saturday mornings with her husband and son, and she looked equally so by my curb in black, waiting for the ride that would take her to their funeral.

Though I'd never met Lisbeth, I had met her husband. Before he died, Miles Pomeroy was second trumpet for the Boston Symphony Orchestra, and although I didn't have any professional ties to him, I'd met him at two charity events widely supported by the classical music crowd. He played well enough to land some solo recording contracts, and I in fact own two baroque CDs with his name on their covers: one Haydn, one Handel. He had a bright trumpet voice, almost too orgiastic for my taste, but I sometimes heard that voice in the scores I wrote for the instrument—which, in my line of work, is a compliment.

Miles and his son, Matthew, had died on the third Sunday in June in a car accident on their way home from an air show. Like many six-year-olds, Matthew liked the old military planes—how they ducked and dodged, their fiercely painted faces. Someone of driving age evidently shared Matthew's passion, and was looking at the sky instead of at the road when his yellow bread truck slammed head-on into the Pomeroys' vintage BMW. The impact crushed Miles's chest against the steering column and threw Matthew, who had been kneeling by the open passenger window, through the loops of his seat belt and onto the road, where he was run over by the bread truck. I didn't hear about this firsthand, but second or third. By the time I learned the details—by the time I could imagine Matthew on the road, trying to roll out of the way before being crushed to death—the story was just another neighborhood fact that shocked no one. It had gotten so abstract that people wondered aloud whether Miles or Matthew had the easier death.

Fourteen months after her tragedy, Lisbeth succumbed to the frenzy of summer and finally let herself wear bright colors again; she maintained, with admirable stoicism, a cheerful public demeanor. She smiled at strangers more—so many people whose names she didn't know had been so kind to her lately—and she smiled at me with a vague sense of recognition when we saw each other on our morning walks. If I got an early start on mine, or Lisbeth and her dog a late one on theirs, we'd cross paths in the northwest corner of the Public Garden.

On the last Friday in September, feeling remorseful and embarrassed at the feeble advances I'd made toward a flutist the night before, I made a special effort to bump into Lisbeth so I could recalibrate my relationship with the female half of our species. The first emotion I felt toward her that morning was guilt:

in all the months since I'd learned about the accident, I hadn't managed to come up with even a single hackneyed condolence for her. And if I had any intention of offering one, I needed to do it that Friday; my perpetually soon-to-die parents in Michigan had wheedled an extended visit from me, for which I would leave the next morning, and it would be two or three months before I had the chance to see Lisbeth again.

I wanted to do what was good, right, and neighborly. Perhaps more importantly I wanted to see Lisbeth in the remnants of her mourning, since by the time I returned she might be remarried, in which case condolences would no longer be appropriate. I brought along a newspaper and some troublesome notation for a Béla Bartók-meets-Philip Glass string quartet I'd been revising, which I carried around constantly in the hope that its problems would resolve themselves without any real effort from me.

This happens to composers sometimes. You're sitting someplace or walking someplace and you hear a voice, a random combination of car horns and footsteps, and a musical idea overtakes you. Receptivity to randomness solves the problem you've been gnawing on for weeks, months. Physicists and mathematicians report this same phenomenon. I found a park bench where I could see Lisbeth coming from any direction, set the sheet music on my lap, and readied my pencil. But she never showed—some holdup, a headache, an unusual day. I had to make up for hitting on the flutist by being unbearably kind to a twenty-year-old violin student I met on the flight to Detroit.

I got used to the snow in Michigan and welcomed the fresh cover of whiteness that greeted me when I returned to Boston in early December. My parents had remained alive for the whole of my visit, and in fact crept toward death more slowly than ever. They attributed their longevity and robust health to using as little heat as possible in the winter and taking long morning walks every single day, regardless of the weather. This shamed me into continuing, and even lengthening, my strolls in the Public Garden. I left early my first morning out, hoping to finally offer my condolences to Lisbeth, and sauntered gently under the trees so I could feel the fresh snow glide off the branches and tickle my face.

Lisbeth did come, and she looked as magnificent as ever — this time in green rubber boots and red mittens. She walked up the path with her big, shaggy golden retriever, and looked in exactly the same phase of mourning as when I saw her last. Judging from her walled-in facial expression and the marching pace of her walk, she appeared to have found no new husband. She failed to notice me despite my too-enthusiastic wave, then detoured across the grass onto a flower bed. There the dog walked back and forth and sideways like a circus Chihuahua, closely guided by Lisbeth's taut leash and insistent voice.

I had no idea what I'd just witnessed, but when the retriever finished its dance, Lisbeth gave him a cookie and they continued their walk as if nothing out of the ordinary had occurred. As our paths crossed seconds later I flashed her a sympathetic smile, and she stared back the way you do at acquaintances whose names you can't recall.

"Beautiful snow," I said, and we both sort of stopped — that half-stopping, half-sideways shuffle people do when they feel inclined to have a conversation, but don't know each other well enough to justify it.

"Absolutely," she replied with her eyebrows raised in assent, but offered nothing more as she walked past me. From up close she looked about thirty-six, which would have made her seven years my senior, and I briefly indulged in the fantasy of being her second husband. Not in a merely sexual way, but in the habitual, day-to-day way that husbands and wives interact. Doing small favors for each other, either by request or by surprise. Hustling out the door on some days, deciding not to hustle out on others.

It was a good fantasy, and Lisbeth fit the role of my wife perfectly. I walked over to the flower bed to see what the dog had done, and found that the unmistakable letter *M*, four feet by four in canine footprints, had been trampled into the snow.

• • •

The next morning I got a later start on my walk and saw Lisbeth and her dog perform the ritual again, this time from a more discreet distance. Another *M* in the snow, more perfect than the last, and another cookie in reward. I marveled over Lisbeth's persistence. How long had it taken her to train that dog? How many times had I seen them doing this before the snow came, and never noticed the letter? I hurried to catch up, but slipped on a bit of ice twenty feet away.

"Excuse me!" I was saying as I threw an arm in the air to keep my balance. Lisbeth turned just in time to catch my odd pose — I must have looked like I was hailing a cab. The dog fastened its eyes on me for a wary moment, then started wagging its tail.

"Hello?" Lisbeth's voice was as tenuous as her recognition of me the day before.

"I can't help but notice what you're doing with your dog."

"What I'm doing? What do you mean?" She pulled the retriever closer to her.

"The *M*, there in the snow. I saw it yesterday, I saw it today."

"Oh, that's nothing. It's just a little game we play." Lisbeth swallowed hard, looked at me like a child about to be scolded, and leaned down to pat her dog's head. "Isn't that right, honeypie?" she asked it.

"We're neighbors, aren't we?" I cocked my head, feigning uncertainty.

"Yes, I know. You're Clay. You're a—" She couldn't remember what I did for a living, or couldn't bring herself to say it.

"I'm a composer." I hated being called Clay, but decided to let Lisbeth do it. Maybe Miles had passed my name on to her in its short, annoying form. "I, uh, knew your husband. Just briefly. I was sorry to hear—"

"That's all right." The dog strained to greet me, but Lisbeth pulled it back. She didn't want to talk about her husband. "This is Knuckles. He's a he."

"Knuckles, huh?" I stepped forward and crouched down to pet his shaggy skull. "Knucklehead's more like it!" I roughed up his ears and let him play tug of war with my coat sleeve. Knuckles was a man's dog, and obviously missed having a man around to roughhouse with him.

"I'll let him go," Lisbeth said, then she unlatched his collar and watched him jump around in the snow with me. I felt ridiculous on my hands and knees, growling at someone else's dog, but Knuckles required a certain kind of attention that I needed just as badly to give. I suppose I'm unlike most classical music types in that I feel a childlike joy in the roughness of life, and it's difficult to find people in my crowd who can share that joy with me. But Knuckles shared it in spades. He got his canines into my gloves and tore holes in them until the stuffing came out. He caught the hard-packed snowballs I threw his way, sometimes with a bit of zip on the toss. He'd seemed so boring to me when he stood beside Lisbeth, but he was a great dog now that he had a man to play with again.

"He's crazy about you," Lisbeth said when Knuckles and I got tuckered out. She called him over to reattach the leash, and I brushed the slobber off of my coat with snow. "Play with him anytime, please. He misses his daddy and his brother, poor thing."

"Is that what the *M* stands for?"

"Yes, both of them. Miles and Matthew." Lisbeth didn't want to talk about the *M* either. Instead she looked at my clothes, which were soaked through in spots from my wrestling match with Knuckles. "You're all wet. Are you heading home? I have hot cocoa."

"Heading downtown," I told her. "Picking up some copies."

"Then tomorrow, maybe. Or you can stop by. Do you know where we are?"

"Yes, I do." I felt tempted to call her ma'am right then, but didn't want to forfeit my right to fantasize about being her husband.

"Good. Bring tennis balls, if you have them."

"I will. Nice meeting you."

"You too." She pointed at me and squinted with one eye. "Clay, right?"

"Clayton." I winked at her—very stupid, something I hadn't done to a woman since I was an undergrad—and gave a thumbs-up to Knuckles, who lunged back toward me momentarily.

Thus ended my Lisbeth Pomeroy interaction for the day, and I headed downtown even though I had no copies to pick up and no actual business there. Stupid lie! Idiot deception to avoid hot cocoa with a woman I could adore! Instead I spent an hour in Filene's Basement shopping for a new pair of gloves, then left my old ones on a park bench—a slightly damaged gift for the cold-fingered homeless. I bought a bagel I didn't need and fed pieces to the pigeons, wondering how Knuckles felt about pigeons. Whether he ignored them, or ran away from them, or tried to chase and eat them.

At the tail end of my downtown trip I bought a can of tennis balls, which I left on my back porch overnight so they'd lose their disgusting new rubber smell. I didn't take a walk the next morning, but instead waited by my office window for Lisbeth to come back from hers. I gave her five minutes to get her boots and coat off, and maybe start up a pot of cocoa. Then I walked over, got buzzed in, and found Knuckles waiting for me at the open door of 3B.

"Hey Knucklehead," I said as I walked in without a proper invitation, and I roughed up the dog even more than I had the day before. Knuckles loved it, and he loved the tennis balls too. Later on Lisbeth said he liked them best when they were brand-new and rubbery smelling, so I didn't tell her about the night they spent on my porch. I did apologize to Knuckles for it, though, when Lisbeth went to finish making the cocoa that she had, indeed, started. Soon she glided into the living room with two hot mugs and sat down on her couch to watch me play with Knuckles. I broke from wrestling to sip my cocoa, raise my eyebrows, and hum at the taste in approval.

"Let me ask you a dumb question. Why Knuckles?"

"It was Matthew's first word, believe it or not." She pointed to a photo on the wall of her son riding Knuckles bareback. "One of Miles's brothers came over, and he kept on trying to get Matthew to say *uncle*. But the best he got was *nuncl*. The next day we got the dog, and Matthew kept on saying the word to it. *Nuncl*."

Knuckles got a little too rowdy with me, and Lisbeth sent him to his bed on the back porch for a time-out. I washed my hands and joined her on the couch, where we enjoyed her cocoa and talked about the neighborhood. My eyes roved around the room and found a variety of half-finished artwork: pen and ink drawings, acrylic paint on glass, big charcoal sketches. Her work showed skill, the pen and ink drawings especially, but they had an aimless, scattered feel to them that I wanted to attribute to her mourning. I wanted her to be an artist whose personal loss had dammed up the flow of her creativity, and I wanted to be the man who blew that dam apart for her. Savior complex, I know.

"Did you do this kind of thing before the accident?" I asked.

"A little bit. I'm just a dilettante, though. It helps me relax."

"Nothing wrong with relaxing." I stood and walked over to an intriguing charcoal sketch. It showed a harsh mountain land-scape full of crevices and dark gray skies, but the quality of the lines broke down when I looked at it up close. A pen and ink piece had finer, more coherent lines and a rural, Vermontish fla-vor. It showed a farm couple embracing, with a sledgehammer on the ground beside them and a small flock of sheep safely behind a wooden fence. It was hokey but well-executed, and I liked it in spite of my universal snobbishness about the arts. I glanced at Lisbeth, who stared out the window as soon as our eyes met.

"Do you have a name for this one?"

"Finished Pen," Lisbeth said, only half looking back at me. "I like to think he called her out to tell her it was done."

"You *like to think?*"

"It's from an old picture, around nineteen-ten." She stood and handed me a photo album that she pulled from a bookcase. It was full of old family pictures, but as I flipped through I never saw the same face twice.

"Is this your family?" I asked.

"No, no." Lisbeth waved the question off. "I go to flea markets, garage sales. People find these pictures in their attics and they don't even know who they're of. Grandparents are dead, parents are dead. I've got a whole closet full of them, and these are the best."

"Interesting." But it was more than interesting. Inspired, maybe even brilliant, something I could apply to my music if only I had the imagination. I wanted to stroke Lisbeth's hands and tell her she was a genius, and I almost did. My hands reached out toward hers at waist level, as open and empty as my mouth. I could even see the electricity that would pass between our skins when we touched—a bright cobalt blue that flashed all the way to our elbows. Before I could reach out all the way to her, Lisbeth picked up our cocoa mugs and headed into the kitchen to refill them.

"It started with family pictures, though," she said as she handed my mug back to me. We went on with our conversation as if my reach had never happened, and I almost threw myself on the floor to thank Lisbeth for ignoring it.

"Your family?"

"No." She thought about sitting down, then changed her mind and poked through some of her charcoal sketches. "Miles had a big family, and I did portraits as gifts. Birthdays, Christmas, graduations. But since the accident I don't do so many of those."

"You're not still in their lives?"

"We try, but all that trying shows. It's easier to let things go."

I felt Lisbeth stop breathing and clench her body tight—her elbows hugged her ribcage so hard that her hands shook. I knew it could turn into a mushy scene at any moment: the young widow crying on my shoulder, the love song that would never get finished because it felt too heavy with sadness and *want* right from the very first note. She stood there staring at me, her eyes bulging and instantly red from holding back tears. But Knuckles saved the day when he rushed into the living room, tail wagging, and dropped one of his new tennis balls at her feet.

"Go get it!" she said, and kicked it hard into the kitchen. Knuckles raced after it but fell on the tile, sliding on his hip awhile before he scrambled up and went back to chasing. Lisbeth and I had a good laugh over him.

"I'm sorry about a minute ago," she said when Knuckles came back with the ball. "It's still hard sometimes."

For the next two weeks we walked together almost every day, and I'd go over to Lisbeth's condo for cocoa afterwards. We'd talk about my music, about the generous three-year grant I'd been awarded, about the generous aunt whose condo I rented at only the cost of her mortgage. We'd talk about Lisbeth's art, about her stellar tennis career at Wellesley, about the cello she used to play but sold when she became a widow, and finally about Miles and Matthew. I saw hundreds of family pictures, held Miles's trumpets, heard the stories behind all of Matthew's toys that Lisbeth couldn't bear to get rid of yet.

I used to think that being a shoulder to cry on meant sitting comfortably next to someone and feeling them go slightly limp in your arms, maybe dripping a few tears onto your shirt. I was wrong—being a shoulder to cry on means you get soggy through and through. Lisbeth cried on my shoulder as she stood next to me, cried on my chest as we embraced, cried on my back while I sat at her dining room table. She cried in every possible position, soaked me with more tears than I thought a human being could hold. Once she almost choked me on the couch—she'd gotten both arms around my neck and confessed how she imagined Matthew's death every night. She couldn't get to sleep unless she pretended to be him, felt his last living moment as the wheels of the oncoming bread truck rolled over his chest.

"It's never the same feeling," Lisbeth said. "Sometimes it's panic, sometimes it's sadness for all he's lost, or he feels sorry for leaving me alone. Or he's grateful he got the chance to be alive at all, and doesn't mind that he died young."

Then she sobbed some more and I smelled her hair and skin,

briny now from all the tears. After that there was nothing else to say, and our post-cocoa crying session ended the same way as all the others: Lisbeth walked me to the door and said goodbye, then hugged me — no kiss — and rested her forehead against my shoulder.

"See you tomorrow," I told her.

"You don't have to keep coming over. I'm not interested in charity."

"I'm not here for charity." I smiled and she looked up at me as if she finally felt ready for a kiss, but neither of us could make the move. I went home and changed my shirt as usual, leaving the tear-soaked one drying on a hanger in my bathroom.

Then I masturbated thinking of Lisbeth. Thinking of giving her another son, a magical child who could never die.

The next day we exchanged Christmas cards and quickly shared rum-spiked eggnog before flying off to celebrate with our respective families. Lisbeth didn't cry and we didn't talk about Miles or Matthew, and I didn't wrestle with Knuckles because she'd already taken him to a kennel. We made no specific plans to see each other when we got home — both of us were uncertain about our return dates, anyway. I let Lisbeth go first, and didn't step out the door until I saw her walk back home with Knuckles.

Perhaps she needed a break from me, or had seen the folly of spending so much time with a man five years her junior (she turned out to be only thirty-four) who had seen comparatively little of life. But in retrospect, it seemed that something needed to cook inside her awhile before she saw me again — desire, self-forgiveness, something I can't name. Something I could put a melody to, a mood and color to. But not words. Don't ask me for the words.

Whatever it was cooked until January 4, when Lisbeth knocked on my door for the first time ever. I sat on my couch listening to a sloppy recording of a piano solo I was working on — something I do with a piece whenever I feel almost finished, with no pencils in sight so I can't muck it up right away—but I didn't feel like turning the stereo off. Lisbeth had a pair of blue terry cloth slippers on her otherwise bare feet, and they were covered with the sludge she'd walked through to get from her brownstone to mine. She stood in the doorway looking cold and uncertain. I'd never been that close to her without Knuckles around.

"Do you want some socks?" I asked her as she came in.

"No. I'm okay." She closed the door behind her, took off her slippers, and paced around barefoot on the hardwood floor without really looking at anything. Without noticing the piano or the piles of books and CDs, or the sheet music cluttered all around. But her brow furrowed at a deep, dissonant chord, and she cocked her head at my speakers.

"What are we listening to?"

"Me," I said, and I didn't wait for her to say anything back. "It's kind of funny without Knuckles, isn't it?"

"Yes, it is." Lisbeth stepped toward me and we hugged in our usual way, with her forehead on my shoulder. Her shaking body made me expect a kiss, and it came, and I let myself fall into it. I told myself I'd wanted that kiss since the day I saw her on the curb in mourning, though in truth I'd only wanted it since the day I first drank cocoa with her. Or was it the snowy day when I met her and Knuckles in the Public Garden? Or the day I waited for her there in September, and she never came?

No matter. At thirty-four Lisbeth Pomeroy should have been, according to all the popular experts, in her sexual prime. But she brought the ghosts of Miles and Matthew into my bed with her, and they created such a force field that I could barely touch her. She made me cover my dresser mirror with a blanket so she couldn't see herself naked, and wouldn't let me near her breasts at all. Having Knuckles around might have relaxed her, I couldn't help thinking. Everything felt rushed and perfunctory, but she insisted.

"I want you close to me," she said. "I deserve that, don't I? Don't you?"

Lisbeth didn't feel up to having an orgasm but wanted me to, and said she was at a time in her cycle when it didn't matter. Whatever she meant by that, it had a rather distancing effect. It was terrible sex, wrong in every way, but in the end Lisbeth thanked me. Not for the act itself, which she agreed had not been ideal, but for the intimacy. She didn't need to tell me that I was the first man she'd been with since her husband died, but she did anyway.

We showered separately, and Lisbeth got under my covers to lay on her side. I nestled in behind her and let her guide my hands and knees into what she considered to be the perfect spooning position. We slept for an hour until Lisbeth woke like a shot — remembering her date that evening with a fellow symphony widow — and hustled home in her wet blue slippers.

That night over the phone, Lisbeth and I agreed upon a new procedure for our morning walks: she would ring my buzzer at seven-thirty A.M. sharp, then stand beneath the window with Knuckles and wait for me to come down. No guesswork, no peeking out the window, no wondering when to get dressed. I welcomed her efficiency, her practicality, and eagerly awaited the start of our new routine.

But the next morning seven-thirty went by, then eight, and Lisbeth still hadn't showed. So I went over to her place, worried that she would either be terribly guilty about sleeping with me or terribly clingy. She was, in fact, making cocoa again. She didn't go for guilt or puppy love, and kissed me on the cheek like we'd been married for years. Then she put Knuckles on the back porch and brought me cocoa on the couch.

"I don't have any regrets about yesterday," she said. "As long as you don't."

"Not at all." I took a big mouthful of cocoa to give myself time to think before I talked. "I'd like to see you that way more often. Go places with you, too."

"You mean like a boyfriend?"

"Aren't we too grown-up for—?"

"No, we're not." She put her finger to my lips. "I like it. *Boy-friend.*"

Our second time in bed — on the couch, actually — went significantly better than our first. Lisbeth worked herself up to a rather spastic orgasm, after which she could barely move, and I brought myself to the quietest, gentlest climax of my life. We reheated the unused cocoa and snuggled under a blanket, laughing and making up fake answers to crossword puzzle questions.

"I wish we were in your bed," I said when we woke up from dozing.

"We'll see about that. I might need to buy a new bed."

It was almost noon by the time we walked down to the Public Garden hand in hand, and we broke our grip only once on the way. We let Knuckles loose and played on the ground with him together, and Lisbeth got her wool coat sopping wet with half-melted snow. It felt like love to me, but I told myself I wouldn't use the word before she did — not even to myself. We made snow angels and Knuckles licked our faces. Lisbeth looked into my eyes for a long time as we lay on the ground, then buried her head in my snow-covered shoulder.

"Thank you," she said, pecking my lips and looking up at the sky. "Thanks."

I figured she was either thanking God for giving her a second chance at love, or me for being her boyfriend, or Miles for loosening his grip on her from the afterworld and letting her have somebody else. But a few seconds later, none of those options felt right. Lisbeth hopped up, put the leash back on Knuckles, and dragged him over to the flower bed one more time. I knew I couldn't distract her from her mission, so I tried to distract Knuckles instead.

"Hey, Knucklehead!" I yelled, tossing a tennis ball toward him. Knuckles lunged to get it, choking himself against Lisbeth's tug, but she completely ignored both me and the ball. There was something intractable about her then, something implacable that I would never be able to understand or accept, and the love affair I thought we could have began to look weird. Began to look one-sided, with me constantly sacrificing my needs to accommodate her dead husband and son. Maybe being selfish about that cost me a chance at what might have become the love of my life, but I wasn't man enough for so much sacrifice. I was just man enough to try taking a useless stand, nothing more.

"Can't you see he doesn't want to?" I called to Lisbeth. "He wants to play ball. He wants to get on with his life."

"That's only because you're teasing him. Turn around! This isn't your business."

I turned away and heard Knuckles yelp as Lisbeth yanked at his collar. I listened for the sound of the dog's feet on the snow, but of course that was impossible to hear from my distance. Instead I heard Lisbeth's sharp, insistent commands, and then the wet shuffling of her feet as she walked further into the park, away from me. She got twenty yards down the path by the time I felt composed enough to catch up with her and speak reasonably. Walking by I noticed the *M* in the flower bed, jagged and lopsided this time.

"Let it go," I told her. "A dancing dog can't bring back dead people."

"Can I have some privacy, please?" Lisbeth snapped back.

"It's not about privacy—"

"Then tell me what it's about, Mr. Professor of Emotions."

"It's about living your life."

"I *am* living my life." She pointed back at the flower bed. "*That's* part of it."

"You might as well get out the Ouija board."

"It's *nothing* like a Ouija board."

"It's *exactly* like a Ouija board. You write letters to talk to dead people."

"Maybe it's more like laying flowers on their graves. Did you ever think of that?" Lisbeth yanked furiously at Knuckles's leash, her mouth bunched down to the size of a nickel. "Of course not. Nobody died on *you.*"

"If you want to leave flowers, I'll go with you every goddamn day—"

"You don't have to swear, Clay."

"I'll do it every goddamn day. But a dancing dog isn't the answer."

"Fine, then." Lisbeth marched off, dragging Knuckles behind her. The dog, who knew the score a lot better than I did, looked pleadingly back at me. But I didn't follow him.

And that was that with Lisbeth Pomeroy—no calls, no notes, nothing. Two weeks later I found myself in a pet shop, picking up some cat food for a friend who'd wrecked his knee playing hockey with kids half his age. I passed a shelf full of dog toys and saw one that Knuckles would love, a psychedelic tennis ball with an extra-fuzzy surface and jangly bells inside. It smelled as rubbery as five regular tennis balls. I bought it and took it home, boxed it and wrapped it, and left it on the front steps of Lisbeth's building while she was out taking Knuckles for his dance. KNUCKLES POMEROY, the tag on the box said. C/O LISBETH POMEROY, 3B. Then I went upstairs to my office window to watch them walk home.

Lisbeth never said a thing about the package. I tried to take my walks in the Public Garden where and when our paths wouldn't cross, but some mornings I still saw her from a distance. I noticed that she'd started to yell at Knuckles more and more. He grew increasingly uncooperative over time, and once she yelled at him so hard she cried. That day, for the first time, she gave up halfway through the M.

It's hard for me to say exactly what happened with the psychedelic tennis ball, since I've never been inside Lisbeth's condo again. I could imagine her keeping the ball in its box for a few days, next to her unfinished art, and finally letting Knuckles have it in a weak and lonely moment. He'd play with it all night long, gnawing on it and then batting it around like a kitten would. Lisbeth would take the ball away from him just so she could get some relief from its annoying bells, and in the morning she'd wake to find Knuckles whining in front of the dresser where she'd hidden it.

I can't say this for certain, of course, but I do know what I heard one afternoon as I walked beneath her back porch in the alley behind our buildings.

"You silly dog," she told Knuckles. "It's just a ball, it won't be fun forever. Just wait, you'll get bored with it."

But Knuckles never got bored with it. Sometimes, walking in that alley, I heard him batting at it on the porch when Lisbeth wasn't home. Whenever I spied them heading out on their morning walks, he inevitably had it in his mouth. Once I found it in the Public Garden, underneath a park bench, and the next day I took it into the alley. I aimed at Lisbeth's back porch, closed my eyes, and hurled that tennis ball like some ancient Greek demigod throwing a javelin.

It bounced against her wall once, then slowly settled on the floor. It never came back down.

Our Last Garage Sale

WHEN YOU LOOK at people too much, they get into your head in ways they shouldn't. My fiancée Shelley and I looked at Kenneth and Margaret Mapleton a lot, partially because they were both gorgeous examples of our species' beauty and partially because we sat in a car with them for two hours every single Friday. We knew Kenneth and Margaret because we carpooled to our office park in San Jose with them once a week — a scheme some do-gooder cooked up to simultaneously save the environment and foster community bonding. Shelley and I liked to call Friday "Superficial Day," because surface is all we ever saw of the Mapletons. Every question we asked got answered with some version of "Fine, and you?" We'd jabber blandly about the consumer goods we wanted to buy and about our fantasy remodeling projects, and every commute gave us enough ammunition to make fun of them for the whole rest of the weekend. Sometimes in front of our friends.

After the first few weeks we took to imitating them on Friday mornings while we got dressed, ate breakfast, and either picked them up or waited for them on our front porch. Shelley liked the way I played Kenneth, with my eyebrows perpetually raised in erotic amusement. I liked the way she played Margaret, with her saucy little mouth and those X-ray eyes that could tell how much your clothes cost from a football field away. Sometimes we got so into our parts that we ended up jumping each other, and had to scramble to get our disheveled, sex-happy selves out the door in time. It always made Superficial Day more tolerable, and we suspected that Kenneth and Margaret did the same thing for the same reason.

"I swear they're half a step away from asking us to do a spouse swap," Shelley told me as we waited on our porch one Friday, straightening our clothes after a quickie in the foyer. "You ever get that feeling?"

"I do." She'd said that once before, but I couldn't think of anything clever to say back either time. Instead I touched her rump and raised my eyebrows the way a man like Kenneth might. "I just don't know whose mouth it'll come out of yet."

Two minutes later the Mapletons pulled up, and we put on our fake smiles as we climbed into their Lexus. I don't know if they had spouse swapping on their minds, and can't speak for Shelley, but personally I couldn't help thinking how savage Margaret would look naked, with her false civility stripped away and her teeth bared in passion. Coming at me with those starry Lauren Bacall eyes, that thick wave of chestnut hair bobbing against her neck, and of course her taut little English duchess mouth.

Shelley must have read my mind, because when I looked at her she flashed me her best imitation of Margaret's lips. I felt that pout slide down from my neck to the bottom of my ribcage, and whether it was Margaret's or Shelley's in my imagination I couldn't tell. Then I looked at the leather on the back of the driver's seat just to escape from that fantasy before it got too familiar. It was nice leather. Kenneth and Margaret were about fifteen years older than us, forty-five maybe, and earned enough to afford both the Lexus and a $3 million house in Los Gatos. He was some kind of software executive, she the corporate communications VP of an arch-rival company—the kinds of things Shelley and I might be doing in fifteen years, if our jobs and respective companies got better. The four of us babbled on about how fine everything was, as usual, then suddenly had the first moment of silence in our five months of carpooling together. I can't even remember how it started, but it was exhausting, humiliating, life-threatening. If I'd known which button unrolled my window, I would have leaned out and screamed at the highway.

"You should come to our garage sale tomorrow," Margaret finally said.

"Garage sale?" Shelley sounded as surprised as I felt. "Are you moving?"

Kenneth smiled at us in the rearview mirror. "We're getting divorced."

I'd never seen anybody so cheerful about it. We watched people our age splitting up all the time, and they tore themselves apart even with only a few years of marriage under their belts. The Mapletons had seventeen.

Margaret turned around and nodded at us, maniacally upbeat. I managed to muster an "Oh!" but couldn't say "I'm sorry" or "How sad" because they didn't seem in need of sympathy. "We're getting divorced"—it was a simple fact, like "The water heater needs replacing" or "We have gophers in our backyard."

"I'll miss our Friday commutes, then," Shelley said, leaning forward to catch both their eyes. She loved to play the conciliator, and I usually loved that about her. But this time I wished she'd stay out of it.

"Oh no," Kenneth told us. "We'll still be neighbors. Margaret's moving down the street to live with a younger man."

"And Kenneth has a little coed moving in to take care of *all* his needs. Isn't that sweet of her? And isn't he *soooo* deserving?"

Kenneth smiled wide and raised his eyebrows, no doubt pondering the endless sex he'd soon be having. The word MINEFIELD flashed across my brain like a big rock headed for the windshield, and I said nothing. I thought about basketball.

"We were never really faithful to each other," Kenneth went on.

"Not even close. So we figured, why bother lying? It got to be *such* a drain to lie."

"And an *incredible* drain to be married when you're lying. Remember that." Margaret wagged a finger at us. "If you're going to start lying, don't bother getting married. Or staying married."

"I'll remember," Shelley said, giggling.

I didn't like the sound of Shelley's giggle, since it felt like a sincere version of her Friday morning imitations of Margaret. I'd never heard her do that laugh as well as she did then. And without wanting to—desperately wanting *not* to, in fact—I felt Kenneth's signature "Ha-huh!" climb up my throat. Try as I might, I couldn't keep it from hopping out of my mouth.

The Mapletons lived exactly 3.4 miles from us, just across the city line. I knew this because Shelley was a contractor and kept track of her mileage for Uncle Sam. We drove my truck over and got there at nine-thirty, and by then people were hauling away bed frames, kitchen appliances, tablecloths, a couch, a loveseat. The neighbors to either side sat on lounge chairs in their front yards, drinking iced tea and no doubt trying as hard as Shelley and me to understand the terms of this divorce. The second our doors closed, Margaret rushed over to greet us looking like she was on pills—Vicodin, Valium, who knows. Her eyes twinkled more than I'd ever seen them, but then again I'd never seen them on the weekend before. She wore a loose blue sundress and a floppy straw hat, and for some reason had four-inch gold spike heels on.

"*Wonderful* to see you!" she cooed. Instead of shaking our hands, she rubbed them between her palms. "Let me tell you the rules. Everything for sale here is something the two of us have bought together, either with joint money or mutual approval. Uh—mutual decision. You know what I mean, you're practically married. You can ask either one of us for a price on something, and if you don't like that price, then you can ask the other spouse. Whoever gives you the lowest price takes your money, unless you like the higher one. I think you'll find the prices reasonable, because we're *very* eager to get this crap out of our lives."

"Okay then!" Shelley opened her eyes wide to make them twinkle too. Margaret took her hand, leaning toward her ear as if ready to suggest that spouse swap at last, but turned around when she heard someone call her name. She slipped away, put an arm around an older man's waist, and give him a price of $35. The man nodded in approval, handed over his money, and walked off with a fancy-looking bread mixer. Margaret forgot about us and moved on to other guests.

"Don't act like her," I said to Shelley. "Please."

"I'm not acting like her," she snapped back. Then she thought about it and said, "If I am, it's in ways I can't help."

"Then God save us all, if you can't help turning into that."

"Give her a break. She's a middle-aged woman getting divorced. You have to let her be miserable."

"That's a chicken or egg situation." Before I had a chance to explain, Margaret was right back on top of us with those twinkly, drugged-out eyes. She leaned in, close and confidential.

"We have some special deals too. Kenneth's been plotting to get rid of some of my things, so I'm plotting to get rid of some of his. Like a couple gets divorced and the wife sells a fifty-thousand-dollar Corvette for five hundred dollars?"

"We've heard of things like that," I said, pulling my lips tight like Kenneth did when he smiled. The only way to get through this garage sale was to be like our hosts and wear their respective masks awhile. Shelley knew it the second we arrived, and I was finally catching on.

"Sounds like fun," Shelley chirped for both of us. Surface, all surface.

"When I wink," Margaret whispered to me just loud enough for Shelly to hear, "make believe you have to use the bathroom, and I'll see you inside."

"Okay," I whispered back. Margaret slipped away again and we looked through all their junk. There was absolutely nothing we wanted, as most of the booty had already been picked over. Serious garage salers show up long before nine-thirty, and the best of the breed can smell a juicy cache from miles away. I fondled a pair of spatulas I thought we could use, but Shelley didn't believe in buying things that might have been in other people's mouths. She scrounged through the books and the furniture, the bric-a-brac, the power tools. I picked up a Herb Alpert CD and Kenneth, swooping past me, stopped to grab my shoulder. He looked jolly as hell in his lavender polo shirt, like a man ready to enjoy a long string of college girls.

"Forty-six bucks for the CD," he said. "See if you can get a better price from the wife."

"Isn't she an *ex*-wife?"

"Not yet. But you can bet as soon as she is, that's what I'll be calling her!"

His eyes twinkled just as much as Margaret's, and I wondered if they were on the same drugs. If they woke up that morning and decided, "Hey, let's get high on Valium for the garage sale!" I watched Kenneth move through the crowd, all smiles, and his jolliness pissed me off—made me question the sanctity of marriage, or even its wisdom. I knew I'd be in a funk for at least a year if I ever broke up with Shelley, and we weren't even married yet. But maybe being married to somebody for seventeen years beats that kind of sentimentality right out of you, to the point where you move on without moping at all. I realized that I had a lot to learn, but wasn't sure how much of it I wanted to learn from Kenneth.

"What are you doing with the stuff that's left over?" I asked him the next time he whizzed by me.

"Oh, there won't be anything left over. If there is, I'll burn it."

"Burn down the house too?"

"Oh, I've thought about that, believe me! Efficient, but inconvenient."

Kenneth grinned and moved on. Across the yard Shelley found something she loved—a full-size mirror with a big thick frame covered in real leopard skin. It looked real anyway. Shelley stared at it and could barely speak.

"I love it," I told her, lunging down to kiss her neck. "A hundred dollars."

"Since when do you name the prices?"

"I'm just saying what I'm willing to pay."

"Oh." She tilted the mirror and caught my eye in it. "They're cute, aren't they? As cute as divorcing people can be?"

"They terrify me."

My voice sounded like it did when we argued—like I had a belt wrapped tight around my chest and couldn't fill my lungs without gasping. Shelley inspected the back of the mirror and nodded in approval. Then Margaret came around.

"Two hundred seventy-five dollars for the mirror," she told us. "Three dollars for the CD."

"Kenneth wanted forty-six," I said.

"Kenneth and I have different opinions about the worth of things." A fleck of spittle flew through the air to emphasize the *p* in *opinions.* "We have different opinions about the worth of each other, which is what all this comes down to. He values himself more than I value him, and I value myself more than he values me. Wow, I got through all that without messing up the words! What a treat!"

All three of us laughed. Maybe she was on downers, since downers can make you stumble over your words. Or Quaaludes, since they were about the right age to have enjoyed Quaaludes back in the day. Margaret cocked her head and scrunched down the whole right side of her face.

"I'm winking at you now, Ed," she told me. "You know what that means."

"Yes, I do." I winked back, just as un-subtly, and took Shelley's hand.

"Meet me inside, as soon as you get a price on the mirror from Kenny."

She looked me up and down, narrowing her eyes to slits, and

headed into the house. Kenneth bounded up the driveway and pointed at the leopard-skin mirror.

"Forty-six bucks," he said.

"Fabulous," Shelley told him. "Sold."

"Keep looking around, I'll put it in your truck." Kenneth's eyebrows, predictably, jumped up at Shelley as he took the mirror and her keys. As he walked down the driveway I could feel her wondering what it would be like to sleep with him—whether he could still be tender after all those years of faithless marriage, whether sex could ever mean more than satisfaction to him, etc.

"Go talk to him," I told her. "If you have to."

Shelley nodded, but didn't follow Kenneth—at least not while I could see her. I headed for the front door full of sexual curiosity, wondering if Shelley knew something I didn't when she said the Mapletons might be up for a swap. Wondering if I'd have to make the first move, or if I could hang around and wait for Margaret to do it. Wondering if Kenneth would have to make the first move, and if Shelley would have to bite on it.

Then Margaret appeared at her front bay window, tapping the glass. I glanced over at Shelley, who was pawing through a box of vinyl albums even though we didn't have a turntable. Then I slid through the front door and followed Margaret's trim, taut calves across the almost empty living room. I must confess that I wanted to pull white silk stockings down over those calves with my teeth, and Margaret must have seen it in my eyes. She stopped at the fireplace, leaned toward me, and laid her palm on my cheek.

"Oh sweetie, I know what you're thinking, but it's not going to be like that for us. I'm all business today." She removed her hand and pointed at a thumb-size green jade Buddha on the mantelpiece who lifted his arms overhead as if holding up the world. "Kenneth's grandmother went to China in nineteen-ten. She brought home two of these, and I'd like you to have one."

"Where's the other?" I asked her.

"That's not your business."

Her voice had such a hard edge all the sudden that I couldn't look her in the eye. And what would I do with Kenneth's Buddha? I saw myself displaying it on *Antiques Roadshow* and listening to some appraiser saying it was worth $800,000—enough to buy our way into Los Gatos, though not quite enough for a house like the Mapletons'. But could I enjoy myself in a house like that if Kenneth's Buddha bought it for me, since I'd gotten it through immoral means?

"Does Kenneth know about this?" I asked Margaret, feeling the smooth whorl of Buddha's left ear.

"Kenneth started it." She shimmied her hips for no discernible reason. "He has to know. Hurry."

Margaret grabbed the Buddha, slipped it into my hip pocket, and pushed me toward the front door. She sneaked out a different one, scrambled around the house, and pretended to intercept me on the front walk.

"See you Friday!" she said, hustling off after somebody else. I got halfway down the driveway before I ran into Kenneth, who handed me Shelley's keys. I put them in the front pocket where his Buddha wasn't. Shelley herself was nowhere to be found.

"Left a little surprise for you in the truck," he whispered, and then he looked away like he didn't know me. I found Shelley talking to a neighbor woman, someone who'd always waved to us from her garden when we picked up Kenneth and Margaret, and I headed over to ease her out of the conversation.

"Was that weird?" Shelley asked me as we walked back to the truck.

"Very." We drove off without knowing what Kenneth had left us. We peeked through the topper's window at some object on top of the leopard-skin mirror: three feet high and one foot wide, covered by a thick gray blanket. For 2.9 of the 3.4 miles home we experienced complete silence, staring ahead like the road might end suddenly and hurl us into an abyss. Then Shelley turned to me so fast it made me jam on my brakes.

"We never gave them any money," she said, pointing at the CD by my thigh.

"We can give it to them Friday."

"I'm not driving in with them on Friday, Eddie. I'm having brain surgery. My mother's having another funeral. I'm getting a leg amputated, something."

I rolled through the last two stop signs, and Shelley didn't yell at me for it like she usually does. For some reason I still can't explain, I backed my truck into the garage and closed the overhead door before we checked out Kenneth's surprise. Didn't want our neighbors to see anything scandalous, I guess.

"You ready?" Shelley asked as we walked around to the back. I responded only by unlocking the topper latch and opening its window. Underneath the blanket was a dead, stuffed German shorthaired pointer, with one paw lifted up and its nose sticking forward to sniff some unseen prey. I knew the breed because my next-door neighbors had one when I was a kid. A brass plaque on the mounting pedestal said, GORDIE 1989–2003.

"Oh my God." Shelley laughed so hard that she doubled over, accidentally banging her forehead against the tailgate. "How can you face a woman when her husband gave you her dead pet dog?"

"I'm going to miss the carpool next Friday too," I said. "I think I'm having an aneurysm."

"I've got tetanus," Shelley replied. "Rabies, too."

"Appendectomy."

"Kidney dialysis."

"Botulism."

"Heart transplant." We laughed until it wasn't funny anymore. Then I pulled the Buddha out of my pocket.

"Look what Margaret gave me." I set it down between the pointer's legs and we stared at our new possessions for a long, silent minute.

"I like them more now," Shelley said, and for a second I thought she was talking about the dog and the Buddha instead of Kenneth and Margaret.

"At least they're honest," I piped in.

"And they've got spunk." Shelley petted the dog's throat, which shocked me because she didn't like dogs or dead things. "I was worried about them. They seemed so bloodless."

"Like Gordie here?"

"Like Gordie. Exactly." Shelley poked her nose forward like the stuffed pointer, then lifted up one paw and panted a little. With that gesture, I got scared of her—not of marrying her, but of her as a person. Scared of us both, actually, because of all the imperceptible things we'd picked up from Kenneth and Margaret without knowing it. Imperceptible spiritual diseases that would fester unseen, then rot our guts completely the instant before we discovered them. Diseases that would hollow out our marriage—if we even made it that far—with lies and infidelity until it got as flimsy as an eggshell.

Shelley headed inside without looking at me and I stayed in the garage, wondering how we'd find out that our marriage was sick. We'd end up in another carpooling scheme fifteen years later, paired up with a young engaged couple in awe of our money and position. We'd have a laugh, remembering Kenneth and Margaret and congratulating ourselves for staying faithful and not ending up like them. But then we'd get casual about that young couple, start confiding in them in ways we shouldn't, and soon we'd start doing the things we thought Kenneth and Margaret were on the verge of asking us to do. Having them over for dinner and drinks. Dabbling in whatever the new drug was. Letting them sleep over some nights, then inviting them for whole weekends. Finally, when becoming our lovers seemed such a natural choice that they could slip into it without compunction, Shelley and I would start giving them the trinkets we'd been stealing from each other for years.

"Keep these," I'd say, handing the gold hoop earrings that Shelley's mother bought for her in Spain to the sweet, vaguely hippyish girl who I loved to sit behind when it was their turn to drive. Hope, let's call her. I'd be in the garage with her collecting firewood—some other garage, twice as big as ours—while Shelley stood in the kitchen teaching her fiancé, Craig, how to make pad Thai.

"Keep this," she'd say, handing him my Communion ring. Her mouth would be close enough for him to kiss if he dared. "A little nothing, just to remember us by."

When I picked my head up and slipped out of the fantasy, I saw Shelley standing by the door to the kitchen with her face slacker than I'd ever seen it. The first thing I thought was that somebody had broken into our house and turned it upside down, stolen everything we had. But it wasn't that. When I walked toward her she threw her arms around my ribcage and hugged the hell out of me. Not crying or sobbing, but not looking at me either. Had she slept with Kenneth already? Once, or more than once? Was this the confession?

"I'm scared," she said, pulling me tighter when I tried to stand up straight.

"What's this about?"

"I'm scared, that's all." Then she noticed that Gordie was staring straight at us from the back of my truck. Without letting go of me, she reached up and closed the topper.

"What the hell do we do with him?" I asked her.

Shelley pulled back from me and shrugged. Then she opened the garage door and sat on my front bumper to stare out at the neighborhood. Cars coming and going, nobody in their yards — typical Saturday afternoon. The question hung in the air, and we couldn't tell if it would get bigger with time or shrivel up, waiting for the right moment to ask itself.

In Flagstaff

I.

"I've always wanted to come back to the desert," Bethany Bristol said from her seat by the window, just above the wing. She craned her neck to see the ground, but the wing's whiteness blocked her view and made her squint.

"Flagstaff isn't the desert, technically," said her fiancé, Nolan Purcell, who rustled his newspaper and aped nonchalance. He almost blew her a kiss to make up for his correction, but held back. They had both lived in Flagstaff in their youths, years apart and without knowing each other, but it had a shared place in their personal mythologies and they always talked about visiting it together. Now, thanks to a funeral, they were on their way.

"Well I think of it as the desert. Don't I have the right?" Bethany scrunched up her face at him, pushing her small, oval glasses up her nose. She threw that question at Nolan often, and it usually served to goad him into conversation even when he acted distant and unflappable. *Of course you have the right*, he might say. *But that's not the issue, is it?* This time Nolan didn't engage, and Bethany passed it off as anxiety over the funeral. Then she caught him staring at the legs of a redhead about his age across the aisle, which seemed a bad sign for their future together. But as always she turned the question away from their life as a couple, which she refused to doubt, and back onto herself instead.

Were her legs as slim and smooth as the redhead's? No. They looked as thick as a rhino's in some outfits, and she had to shave them too frequently for her own taste. In fact she couldn't match the redhead in any individual qualities except intelligence and diligence—in which she could match anyone—and maybe taste in men, as the redhead's husband looked flabby and sycophantic. But at least he didn't stare at other men's wives, so perhaps the redhead's taste in men trumped Bethany's after all.

"Don't I have the right?" she asked again. "To think of Flagstaff as the desert?" She sharpened her goad, believing that Nolan's unflappability was a sham.

"You have the right to think anything." He glanced over to see how angry his stonewalling had made her. Nolan Purcell was a theater man through and through, and enjoyed watching his fiancée get angry because it gave her such great, guileless faces; ten thousand years of acting classes couldn't disguise Bethany's emotions. Every time she looked at him he learned more about the petty, quotidian dramas that, he believed, gave specific meaning to each human life.

For purposes of study Nolan planned to avoid conversation until Bethany's face went through its entire range of irritation. In his head he had a polished metal gauge inscribed with words that led up to *fuming—miffed, perturbed, upset, grumbling, combative,* etc.—and he liked to watch her move from one word to the next. This made her his muse, he had to admit, though playwrights' muses tended to be more glamorous and conventionally beautiful than Bethany. She was not so much a muse of story as a muse of precision, for she zipped between her emotions like a Porsche slicing down a mountain. When one critic noted the "crisp, lightning-quick emotional turns" of his characters, Nolan attributed them to his prolonged exposure to Bethany. Of course he didn't tell her so; that would have ruined everything, made her start overacting her own life. Much better, he decided, if her spirit lived in his plays and she noticed the homage over time, as they grew old together.

Plays—four- or five-character chamber pieces about the impact of grief and family strife on our ability to love—were Nolan's life and art, and Bethany loved him for it despite the fact that his homage to her was not as transparent as he wished. She sensed a hint of herself in all his characters, not just his women, but didn't mind; her passive contribution to his work helped fill the gaping hole of her own creative life. Bethany had abandoned ceramics in favor of graphic design, then abandoned that for a steady middle-management job. Seeing herself embodied on stage prevented her from feeling like a complete artistic failure and a coward.

To be the future wife of an accomplished artist is at least something, Bethany periodically reassured herself, especially when you don't have the guts to be an artist in your own right. Yet she scourged herself for subjugating her own goals to Nolan's despite how well the arrangement worked for both of them. When they first met she was an unemployed grad school dropout and he'd had only one play produced, a hysterical one-act performed in an eighty-seat attic theater in Cambridge that the Harvard types avoided. Two years later they got engaged; by then she had a career and he'd won prizes, been produced eight times in New York, interviewed on NPR and mentioned in *Variety*. Only their travels to his opening nights—London, Brussels, Berlin, San Francisco, and more to come—kept them from setting a wedding date. He needed to stay flexible, he said, to take advantage of the opportunities that his career might never offer him again. And she couldn't disagree.

By the time Nolan glanced once more at Bethany, the polished metal gauge of her emotions had climbed to *perturbed* and slid back down. She looked at the redhead's legs, then glanced at her own. A small bird of inadequacy flew out of her, but she paid it no mind.

"Do you think people will miss your uncle?" she asked Nolan.

Irritation left her quickly, and she often rid herself of it in one small look away—like the one he saw her cast out the window, exactly on cue.

"No more than when he was alive. I don't think he saw people much." Nolan tried to conjure up a face for his uncle Frank, whom he hadn't seen in sixteen years. Frank had spent the last twelve of them in the hills north of Flagstaff, living in a two-room cabin with unreliable electricity and a septic system that constantly backed up. He obsessively read books on railroad history and corresponded with some of the most notable experts in the field. Two of them had been persuaded by Nolan's other uncle, Gerry, to come for the funeral and bid on Frank's collection of railroad books that dated back to 1867. Frank died at sixty-three, unmarried, but Nolan always pictured him with a woman—someone equally slovenly and obsessive, he guessed, who didn't mind the packrats and feral cats that must have plagued the cabin.

"I know what you're feeling," Bethany said. "I had to go to my great-aunt's funeral and I didn't even know her. I just stood around with a bunch of little women like me, and none of us had anything to say except what we were supposed to say."

"That's not how I feel at all." Nolan violently pulled his newspaper open—not his real emotion, just a test of what a character in his situation might do. "I have plenty of things to say. Too many, actually."

They landed at three-thirty and arrived at Uncle Gerry's house, just uphill from downtown, an hour later. Aunt Becky plied the railroad experts with "authentic German" apple strudel and jars of wild honey. She invited everyone to a family dinner, but Nolan declined, citing exhaustion from his travels. He left his father a message to call when he and his new wife arrived, then drove around with Bethany to tour their old stomping grounds and find the hotel that Gerry had booked for them.

The dinner they would miss sounded, in Nolan's imagination, like the discarded first draft of a Harold Pinter play. Bickering mixed with abstractions, intractable people secretly in love with their own flaws, senseless explosions of vaguely directed rage. Nolan often escaped into theater in this way whenever the reality of a situation bored him or made him uncomfortable. The psychologist he saw in college warned him against this habit, but Nolan felt that it drove him deeper into his art. He discussed the issue with Bethany once, years ago, in a vulnerable moment after a run of his one-act was cancelled early. She, not wanting to squash his dreams, supported his right to escape into whatever alternate world made him happy. Now the issue came up only when Nolan dropped everything to observe Bethany in the midst of some mundane task like folding laundry, emptying the dishwasher, or getting dressed. It made her feel alone even though Nolan was just a few feet away.

"I'm not a character," she told him during one such episode in their first year together as she tried on a dress. "I'm real, I'm here. I'm *very* here." She slipped off the dress more theatrically than she intended, and thus became the very character she claimed not to be. She then seduced him with dynamic results — for Nolan wanted nothing more than to make love with a character in a play — and thenceforward reacted to his moments of deep scrutiny in the same fashion.

But at their hotel in Flagstaff, as she tried on dresses, his watchful eye didn't make her feel sexy at all. It made her restless and twitchy, which Nolan no doubt noticed. Bethany had two dresses on the bed: a burgundy one with sleeves too long for Flagstaff in September, and a black one too shiny and slinky for a funeral anywhere.

"You've got other things for tomorrow, right?" Nolan leaned forward as she smoothed out the dresses on the bed.

"Yes," she said, and he expected her to pull more dresses out of her suitcase. But Bethany didn't want to be watched right then; she'd grown up in Flagstaff, at least partially, and pieces of her still lived in town. She'd walked by this hotel as a sixteen-year-old girl, maybe even peeked through their very window, and in honor of that younger Bethany, she wanted a reprieve from being observed.

She sat on Nolan's lap and put her hand on his belly, where he liked to be touched when he felt insecure. Once he smiled, she let her hand slide down between his legs, but the warmth and movement of her fingers did nothing to excite him. Nolan laughed his way out of the moment and pulled his legs sharply together.

"You're sadder about Frank than you know," Bethany said. "You're so quiet."

"No quieter than usual. I'm—"

"Yes, you're quieter than usual. You're scared of something." In Flagstaff, in this place they both sort of came from, she wanted his reality instead of his dramatized lip service to reality. Nolan looked up at the ceiling with half a tear in his eye and let his thighs fall open, and when Bethany's hand rested between them again he looked at it as if it were a rubber prop that had dropped there randomly. Bethany moved away from his chair and slowly pulled on the black dress. Languorously, even. He watched her smooth it over her body until his breathing settled.

"I don't want to end up like him," Nolan eventually said. "All alone, hardly talking to anybody. I could end up like that, if I'm not careful. Don't you think?"

"No," Bethany replied, even though she had never met Uncle Frank. She slipped the dress back over her head, pulling it off as sensuously as it went on. "You couldn't be, not with me around. It'll never happen."

II.

Nolan's father called to say he wouldn't get to Flagstaff until nine-thirty or ten—too much to do in Phoenix, running further behind every minute. So Nolan and Bethany went looking for the perfect place to eat, stopping at a little bookstore downtown during a break in their search. Nolan always checked out bookstores wherever he went, and he tried to pass this off as curiosity for the local culture. But his college psychologist had discovered—and Bethany had realized on her own after six months of dating him

—that Nolan hid in bookstores the same way he hid in his theatrical imagination. Bethany tried to shake him of this habit, but he refused to discuss it and eventually to even acknowledge it. If she didn't like bookish men, he suggested to her more than once, she never should have agreed to marry one.

Bethany didn't feel like fighting over the bookstore escapism issue this time, so she let Nolan check the miniscule theater shelves for his plays while she poked through the sections that annoyed him most: self-help, Eastern religions, New Age philosophy. As she flipped through a book comparing the lives of Buddha, Jesus, and Krishna, a man behind her said, "Melanie?" in a voice so overjoyed that she wished it were her name instead of her older sister's. Only her cousins and aunts, who had difficulty distinguishing the many short, bespectacled females in their family from one another, ever called her Melanie.

"Sorry." Bethany turned around with the book still open. The man had already reached a hand toward her left shoulder—a rough hand, hard with calluses, but kind nonetheless. She glanced up at his face only long enough to let it register, then looked back at the hand and watched it pull away slowly, ashamed it had ever reached out at all. It was a warm, electric hand, and as it disappeared into his pocket she felt the air around her fall back into a disappointed hum.

Then she looked up at the face again—a beak of a nose, cheeks scarred by years of acne, two days of beard stubble, full lips, black hair thinning on top and curling long in back. His blue eyes looked straight through her the way Nolan only wished his could. Around his waist he wore a red apron filled with markers and pens.

"But I know you." His voice, resonant and deep, rumbled in her chest and belly. "You're the kid sister. Beth, isn't it?"

"Bethany." She smiled because she knew him too. Her sister, four years older, had dated him the year she went to college in town at Northern Arizona University. "You're?—"

"Michael Conway." He held out his hand again, but it was a

perfunctory gesture this time and Bethany felt none of the previous electricity. She shook it as she would the hand of a potential business associate. "You look just like Mel did, way back when. The way you stand up so straight like that. It's crazy."

"We're sisters," Bethany said, and shrugged. "What can I say?"

Conway stared a second too long at Bethany's hands and lips. "How is Mel?"

"Doing well. She's in law school in Baltimore."

"Good for her. You live there too? What brings you back?"

"No, I'm in Boston. My fiancé's uncle has a funeral tomorrow, so I guess it's time to meet the family. Finally!"

Conway's cheeks dropped. "Is it Frank Purcell?"

"Yes, that's him." Bethany cocked her head and Conway imitated her. Almost everything about her reminded him of Melanie — the cocked head, the tautness of her skin, the thrown-back shoulders, the way her glasses slipped down her nose, the mouth that cared so much about what other people thought of her. "Did you know him?"

"Sure, everybody knew Frank. I don't know what your fiancé told you about him, but he was a character."

"They weren't very close. It's one of those family reunion funerals."

"Gotcha. Is it Nolan, this guy you're marrying?"

"Nolan, yes." Bethany couldn't feel her feet on the ground for a moment. Conway knew so much about her, and she knew nothing about him.

"I remember him. Maybe thirty-five now. Glasses, above it all, can't fight, actor."

"He had laser surgery. And he's a playwright now."

"Any good?"

"Yeah, pretty good." Her ribcage tightened for fear that Nolan might have heard her faint praise. "He's here in the store, actually."

"That's nice." Conway suddenly realized that he had her cornered, and backed away half a step. "You're here long?"

"Three days. We leave Sunday morning." Bethany spotted Nolan across the store, not even noticing her conversation. "So you've been here in Flag all this time?"

"Went out to California awhile to get a Ph.D. But yeah, this is home."

"A Ph.D., huh?"

"Didn't seem like the type, did I? I teach at NAU—history, thinking for freshmen. Part-timey stuff."

"And you work here too?"

"I fill in for buddies, cash under the table." He caught Bethany looking away and followed her eyes to Nolan. "So that's what No-lan Purcell turned into, huh?"

"That's him." Bethany looked down without wanting to. It was only the second or third time she'd felt embarrassed over Nolan in public; he looked so slight across the bookstore, too insubstantial and lost in himself for her to ever lean on.

"Well tell him Conway remembers him. I have to get back to work." He patted his apron but didn't move.

"Nice to see you again," Bethany said.

"I'd love to hear more about Mel. Stop by, I'm here all week-end." He snapped his fingers and pointed at her—a thick index finger that came toward the middle of her chest but didn't touch it. "Oh, but I'll see you at the funeral. How'd I forget that?"

They waved and said goodbye and Bethany went back to the book in her hand. It fell open to a section on Krishna and she read the words, but couldn't make sense of them. All she felt was Mi-chael Conway's finger thumping against her breastbone—which hadn't happened, of course. Hadn't even come close to happening.

Bethany didn't tell Nolan about meeting Conway; she wanted to be patient, to be the observer instead of the observed, to watch Nolan react when he saw Conway at the funeral. As they resumed their search for the perfect place to eat, Nolan got a call from his father that changed the tone of their evening. Apparently he wouldn't get into town until ten-thirty or eleven, and the best he could do was a drink at the hotel bar.

"Sure, Dad," Nolan groaned. "Call me when you're here." He then proceeded to bitch about his father for hours—years of let-downs, constant bailing out on commitments. Bethany had heard it all before, though admittedly never in such concentrated and vehement form, so her mind was free to drift toward Michael Conway. How confident and happy with himself he seemed despite his ugly pitted cheeks, despite the fact that he had no real career. Teaching part-time at his hometown college and working under the table in a bookstore—she couldn't imagine Nolan doing that without being three times as self-righteous about his playwriting as he was already. But failing to doggedly pursue his career prospects didn't seem to bother Conway at all, and that fact bothered Bethany. It was a slap in the face to everything she'd taught herself to believe about effort, diligence, success. Ambition, drive, motivation.

All things that Nolan's father, Greg, had plenty of. He finally rolled into the hotel bar at eleven-fifteen, though his new wife, Caroline, felt too exhausted from the drive to join him. Greg talked loud, wore a Rolex, had four diamonds embedded in his platinum wedding ring, and splashed on his cologne as liberally as a second-rate TV mobster. Aside from their physical resemblance—noses, juts of jaws, the way they folded their hands—father and son seemed to share nothing at all.

"So what do you do?" Greg asked Bethany after forty minutes of jabbering about himself and Caroline.

"Educational consulting," she told him. "We go into school districts and analyze their testing metrics, do back-end assessments on the relationship between high school grades and college performance. Things like that."

"Now *there's* somebody who could take over the business," he told Nolan while jerking his thumb at Bethany. Greg's company made heavy-duty hoses and clamps for sewage treatment plants; he'd started it from scratch and it was now worth $18 million. "It's taking you someplace? You're happy doing it?"

"I'm a pretty happy person in general." As soon as the words left Bethany's mouth she wanted to pound the table and kick herself. She was actually a borderline unhappy person who had learned very young how to fake a smile. The realization came to her in Conway's voice—stern but gentle, never judging and never scolding. A voice that knew she lied to herself all the time, but that also believed she would come around to the truth without needing to be badgered about it every waking moment. And badgering was what Nolan did—what Nolan's face did, hovering close by in her imagination, sneering and judging and trying to shame her into change.

"Happy's good," Greg said. "You balance out my son here. Little broody Nolan, still the same kid he always was."

"Come on, Dad. Shut up."

"Oh, gimme a break." He leaned confidentially toward Bethany. "You can't tease this kid now that he's been in the *New York Times*. Probably the *Berlin Times* too, or whatever they call it."

"No really, Dad." He put on a fake New York accent. "Shut! Da fuck! Up!"

Nolan made a hand gesture that Bethany didn't catch, and suddenly the two men were laughing and clinking glasses, hip to hip in the booth with their arms around each other's shoulders. She drank a second piña colada and laughed when it seemed like she was supposed to, and pretended not to notice when the straps of her slinky black dress fell off her shoulders.

III.

Uncle Gerry hadn't given many details about the memorial service—just an answering machine message with date, time, address—and Nolan, nearly as estranged from Gerry as from Frank, didn't ask for more. So he and Bethany were quite surprised to see a line of mourners spilling out the door of the funeral parlor—college kids, skate punks, railroad men with big mustaches, moms holding babies, the entire Flagstaff city council, three photographers, two videographers. Nolan and Bethany had a hard time getting through the line to the seats they were sure had been saved for them.

"We're family," Nolan said to the people they squeezed past, or "Frank's my uncle." They found no reserved seats at the front of the hot, acrid room, but noticed Greg beckoning them over to a spot on the floor. Caroline, blond and perfect and barely forty, smiled at them from behind her lipstick. Bethany smiled back and looked for Conway, but there were hundreds of faces to contend with and she didn't have a hope of finding his.

"You're late!" Greg whispered, mock-whacking his son on the arm as he sat. "I had no idea this many people knew Frankie."

"Me neither," Nolan said, and then a bewildered Uncle Gerry stepped toward the podium. A man in a white coat and gloves, who looked more like a lab tech than a mortician, went behind the coffin for a moment, and his hands appeared to float awhile above the lid's lifted edge. Nolan couldn't figure out what he was doing, but the image etched itself onto his theatrical memory. Gerry tapped the microphone and the crowd pinched toward the front, filling up the aisles all around.

"I don't think the fire department would like this much," Gerry said, pointing to the aisles. "But I'm sure they'll speak up if they get antsy. Right?" A group of firemen whooped and pumped their arms, which made everyone laugh and loosen up. Gerry gave out two deep sighs that everybody heard.

"I know a lot of you feel like you knew Frank real well, and I'm not going to say you didn't. I'm not going to stand up here and tell you I knew him any better than you just because I was his brother. A lot of you out there—like the kids he played checkers with out on the plaza—probably saw a side of Frank I haven't seen since I was seven or eight. That's what happens with families sometimes, and I just regret I didn't get a chance to see the same Frankie you did. Or didn't take the chance, is more like it. But now he's gone, and since I didn't own the man in life I won't try to own him in death. There's a lot of people in this room who want to talk about the Frank Purcell they know, so since this is the Wild West I'm just going to declare anarchy here, and let people come up and do that. Sorry if you were waiting for a big speech."

Then he waved to a small, balding man in a gray suit who turned out to be a trustee of the Northern Arizona University museum, where Frank had volunteered for two decades. A history scholarship, he said, would be established at NAU in Frank's name. Then came the mayor of Flagstaff, who added a posthumous civic award to the two Frank had already earned. Two women who had been his on-and-off girlfriends over the years came up and cried into the microphone together, praising him for his patience and the constancy of his love.

"Well it didn't feel so constant when he was giving it to *you*," one of them said, and the crowd howled. One of the railroad historians came up—the one with the inside track on the books, apparently—followed by a priest who'd been kicked out of the Catholic Church and a vagrant who called himself Tommy. The vagrant said Frank kept him alive more than once.

"All it takes is a couple cans of soup!" he shouted. "A couple fuckin' cans!"

Tommy had to be helped from the podium in tears. Finally Uncle Gerry took the mic again, said he thought Frank would be embarrassed by now, and asked the family to come up and pay their last respects. Bethany didn't feel like family, and of course she officially wasn't yet, but she went along with Nolan and knelt beside him in front of the coffin. It was the first look she got at Uncle Frank—a wild, scruffy man with long gray hair who bore no resemblance to his brothers or his nephew. Next to Nolan were his father and Caroline, followed by Gerry and Becky. At the other end, Nolan's cousin Jake knelt next to a woman Bethany had never even heard about, so she didn't feel so awkward being a stranger up there.

"Amen," Gerry said after a while, and they all stood up and held hands. Bethany had only Nolan's to hold as they took turns stepping forward to make a last silent prayer or wish over the body. Nolan wished for happiness forever with the woman he loved; he did not, however, state the name of any woman in particular, and didn't think of Bethany until he'd already stepped back. When

Bethany stepped up she prayed that Nolan would have the courage to leave her. She'd asked for that only once before, at a Chinese wishing well in Los Angeles, and since it felt like the same basic idea she threw an imaginary penny into Frank's coffin with a quick, barely perceptible flick of her wrist. Wasn't that a tradition somewhere, throwing pennies into a loved one's coffin? Ireland, Africa? Nolan would know, or at least be able to make up some credible bullshit. She imagined Conway catching that flick of her wrist—all those people in the room, and he'd be the only one who noticed it.

Bethany felt sweat trickling down her back, since she had the too-hot burgundy dress on. Then Uncle Gerry walked forward, pushing the group toward the podium to make a receiving line. Greg, who stood in the middle with his shiny Phoenix face and Phoenix suit, looked as out of place in Flagstaff as he would on the steppes of Mongolia. The first pack of mourners were respectable adults who shook everyone's hand and muttered, "I'm sorry," or "My sympathies," to the out-of-towners, but the line got younger and more ragged halfway through—skate punks, homeless-looking types, blue-collar folks who didn't trust people in fancy clothes. Most of them talked only to Gerry, Becky, Jake, and his girlfriend. Some people slid their palms across Nolan's and Bethany's and mumbled, but few looked them in the eye.

That trend ended, though, when Michael Conway came through the line dressed exactly the way Bethany had seen him the day before—sandals, worn chinos, a button-down shirt that probably hadn't been ironed in years. Only the red bookstore apron was missing. He hugged Gerry's family and exaggeratedly shook Greg's hand, though Greg didn't appear to recognize him at all.

"Hi," Conway said as he and Nolan shook hands. "Remember me?"

"No, sorry." The set of Nolan's jaw revealed his lie.

"Michael Conway. You were a senior when I was in tenth grade. Your parents were getting divorced or something."

"Right. How's it going?"

"Doing great. Loved to play checkers with your uncle. He missed you, talked about you all the time. He heard about your plays."

"I didn't even know he played checkers. I had no idea about any of this." Nolan swooped his arms out as wide as he could without hitting anybody.

"He was a hell of a guy. I used to bring him to my history classes, have him do lectures about the railroads."

"So you're teaching at Flag High?"

"No, at NAU." Conway turned to Bethany with his lips pulled tight. "Please say hello to Melanie for me," he told her. "Tell her I have great memories."

"I will. I'm sure she does too."

Then the people behind Conway started pushing him forward. "I'm holding things up, I guess. See you at the ball field."

"Ball field?" Bethany asked.

"Yeah. There's a picnic and a softball game. After you folks bury him."

Bethany said, "Oh," and enthusiastically shook the next few hands that reached toward her. After seeing her chat with Conway, the locals treated her like a real human being instead of some anonymous out-of-towner. They smiled at her, and she gave big, round smiles back to them in memory of the full-faced girl she'd been the last time she had her feet on the ground in Flagstaff.

"I'm sorry, man," a scraggly skate punk told her.

"Don't mention it," Bethany said back with a wink. The skate punk couldn't figure out what she meant, and neither could she.

IV.

All Bethany did during the actual burial—Episcopal blurring into New Age—was fume about what a horrible creep Nolan had been to Conway. *So you're teaching at Flag High?* he'd said, as if Conway could never be anything more than that and only he, the great Nolan Purcell, had the talent to get out of Flagstaff and make something of himself. Bethany wanted to see a war between the pompous creeps and the real people, and she wanted to be the one who started it. A war between assholes like her fiancé, who always found some imaginary way to be better than the people next to them, and genuine human beings like Conway who were happy being themselves.

Bethany worried about what camp the world would put her in, though, because everything about her indicated that she was a pompous creep too. The way she talked to the people who sold her things, the houses she imagined living in, the way she folded her clothes. The man she'd chosen to marry, the other men she'd chosen to bed down with before Nolan came along. So she had to be careful about starting that war.

"Are you okay?" Nolan whispered to her as the pallbearers — Gerry, Jake, and four locals — ceremonially lowered the coffin.

"It's a funeral, Noly. I'm emotional."

Nolan nodded, squeezed an arm around her waist, and whispered that he loved her. Despite the gesture Bethany reconsidered her decision to marry him, citing his reluctance to sacrifice even a moment of his precious career to set a date. She didn't care about the trips to Europe, the New York parties with famous actors who dished out empty promises of working together someday. She could throw it all away and dress in rags to protest Nolan's pomposity, live in a college town like Amherst or even Flagstaff, go back to ceramics or get a Ph.D. in something she'd never even thought about doing before. Not care about her legs, not care that she made less than the median income of a woman with her education, not care if her neighbors had half a dozen dead cars sitting by the curb. Not care about people like Nolan, who kept their noses in the air because they were too scared to come down to earth and get those noses dirty with life.

"It was weird with that guy," Nolan finally said in their orange rental car, following Jake's truck over to the ball field. "The guy with the scarred-up face, Conway?"

"He was Melanie's ex-boyfriend. Don't you remember him?"

"Vaguely. It's hard to see him knowing Uncle Frank, that's all."

"It's not like you knew Uncle Frank." Bethany felt her lower front teeth slide forward, ready to bite. "So it's hard for you to say who'd know him."

"How come you're being so combative?" Nolan banged the heel of his hand against the steering wheel, caught between wanting to fight and wanting to watch Bethany's irritation meter climb all the way to *fuming*.

"I'm not," Bethany said, and that meter lurched up to *combative* immediately. "I'm just saying I don't think you knew him. You're related by blood, that's the only reason you're here. There's no genuine connection."

"That's what this trip's about. Introducing my future wife to her future family."

"But you don't have a family. You have an uncle and a father who hate each other and a new stepmother who looks like a stripper. You don't even know the name of your cousin's girlfriend."

"It's *Sarah*," Nolan hissed as he stopped hard at a red light. Bethany felt overjoyed that he'd finally condescended to lose his cool with her—she'd been waiting their entire relationship for this opportunity. They felt like a real couple at last.

"Okay then. *Sarah*." She snarled it at him, hoping he'd snarl back. "I still wouldn't call that a family. I'm not sure it ever was a family."

"What the fuck do you know about family? You've got your sister, that's it. And a father who sends you Christmas cards."

"And cousins whose weddings I go to. And an aunt I visit in the nursing home. Don't give me that bullshit, Nolan. I know what a family is, and you don't have one, and it worries me."

"It should. End of conversation."

"Yes." Bethany folded her hands and looked away from him for the rest of the drive, but couldn't get her irritation meter down as easily as usual. She got stuck on *fuming*, where Nolan thought he liked her to be, and once she got all the way up there she always lingered longer than he expected. The second they got to the ball field she slammed her door without a word and headed for the rest room just to get some privacy. When she stepped out, Nolan was gone. She saw Conway with a baseball bat, standing between one of Uncle Frank's girlfriends and a tall, teenage boy with pierced lips, and strode up to him.

"I'm sorry what a jerk Nolan was to you at the funeral," Bethany blurted out without even saying hello. "I apologize for him."

"Don't get into the habit." Conway gently tapped the bat against his forehead. "You're really going to marry this guy?"

"Yes." She looked Conway in the eye as feistily as she could. Marrying Nolan felt like the ultimate in self-rebellion—like taking everything she believed she could be and throwing it down a sewer just to prove she had control over her decisions.

"That's stupid. You'll be divorced in a year and a half. You don't know the kind of person you're marrying, or the kind of family you're marrying into."

"That's why I'm here, I gue—" She got cut off by a big collective sigh. Frank's ex-girlfriend had just struck out, and Conway was up next at home plate.

"Ask him about North Flagstaff Dry Cleaning," he said, his body turning away from her. "Just ask him."

"I'll do it tonight."

"No you won't. You don't have the guts."

"You don't know me." As Bethany walked off to find Nolan, Conway strode toward the batter's box; the beer-drenched crowd chanted his name. "Tell me about North Flagstaff Dry Cleaning," she rehearsed as she wandered through a field full of picnic baskets and blankets looking for Nolan. But by the time she found him, he was drinking beers with Jake and pretending to love the family she'd berated him for ignoring. He looked almost like a real person to her, with his tie loosened and the top button of his shirt undone. She even saw him belch, and hoped maybe the trip would make him a tad less uptight. Make him understand human beings a little more—the way they really are inside, the way they behave without someone hovering nearby and pretending they're in a play.

Within half an hour Bethany had obliterated her nerve to tell Nolan off with three cheap beers and a cigarette she smoked on the sly. By then she felt she was blowing everything out of proportion — things would get back to normal in Boston, once they got home where they belonged. Bethany learned that Sarah was a third-grade teacher and Jake coached wrestling part-time on top of his job with the power company. She got unsolicited investment advice from Nolan's father and learned that Caroline had once been in national TV ads for Nivea skin cream. She now worked occasionally as a hand model, though it was hard to keep them looking good with two kids at home — seven and nine, from a first marriage to a wonderful, loving man who'd died suddenly of pancreatic cancer.

Bethany apologized to Nolan for being so cross and leaned her back against his while they sat on a blanket. They stayed like that, feeling each other breathe, long after the rest of the family had moved on. Then they overheard a conversation at a nearby picnic table.

"I walked in there and it was a mess," said a man close to Nolan's age. "Disgusting. We have to do something."

"She left dog food on the kitchen counter so long it dried up and stuck," said the woman who must have been his wife. The other two people in the conversation were older, probably his aunt and uncle. "We had to break it off with a chisel. A putty knife wouldn't even do it."

"You'll never get her into a home," the uncle said. "She's got that in writing."

"I don't want to put her in a home. But the smell horrifies me every time I go over there. Let's just hire somebody to come in and clean once a week, that's all I'm asking."

Bethany craned her neck to catch Nolan's eye, but both of them were closed. "Hey," she said, on the verge of telling him she loved him.

"Shh." He claimed to listen better with his eyes closed, and he was listening hard then. So Bethany listened with him.

"—sure exactly what you can do about it," the uncle said. "You've talked to her already?"

"Three, four times," the younger man replied. "But you can only tell your own mother so much."

"If she doesn't notice the smell, then she thinks there's nothing wrong," added the aunt. "She's a very smell-orientated person."

Bethany tried to get Nolan's attention again. The cigarette and beers had loosened her up, and she rubbed her back sinuously against his. She wanted to go to their hotel and feel him inside her, remind herself that she'd committed the rest of her life to him. "Hey, honey," she whispered.

"Shh!" he hissed back, his teeth clenched. This time he opened his eyes, which glowed with indignation at having his reverie shattered.

"Sorry to interrupt your work," Bethany said, and stood up to leave without knowing where she'd go. She wanted to tell the people at the picnic table that someone was spying on them, that they had to watch what they said because otherwise it would get stolen. Not just their words but their lives too. Nolan Purcell, stealer of life, would yank it out of the air and stuff it down inside himself—where his own life should have been—just so he could have something halfway interesting to write his pompous, melo-dramatic, second-rate plays about.

V.

On Saturday morning Nolan had family things to deal with—the disposition of more assets than anyone knew Frank had, details of that scholarship in his name at NAU, and negotiations with the two railroad scholars for the book collection. Gerry half-invited Bethany, who bowed out charmingly by saying she wasn't quite family yet. She bought Nolan some aspirin and a latté for his hangover, which he'd earned drinking with Jake the night before while she sulked in their hotel room. After driving Nolan up to Gerry's house she ditched the car and walked to an Internet café downtown, where she looked up Michael Conway on the NAU website. She didn't see him attached to any department, but found his name next to three classes on the master schedule.

Bethany felt satisfied—he was who he said he was, if nothing else. She bought an iced coffee and walked around downtown for two hours, scrupulously avoiding the bookstore. Then at eleven-fifteen she dropped in and saw Conway kneeling on the floor, arranging titles in the computer section. The acne pits on his face had become deeper in her mind since she last saw him, and she felt relieved at how shallow they actually were.

"Did you ask him about the dry cleaners?" Conway said when he saw her. No greeting, no smile.

"No," Bethany said. "I'm a little chicken."

"Well I hope it doesn't cost you." He looked down at the floor as if she'd failed her test. "What does Melanie think of him. Has she met him?"

"Yeah. Same as you."

"Well somewhere way down inside you, you have to know it's true."

"It's not very deep inside me at all." She tapped herself on the breastbone, where Conway had almost touched her when they first met. "It's right here."

"Then you're an idiot. You know it's a disaster, but you're still doing it. Tell me how marrying him isn't the most self-destructive thing you can do to yourself."

"Can we talk about this someplace else? You're going to lunch sometime, right?"

"I have lunch at home Saturdays, at noon."

"Fine, I'll get sandwiches. Are you a meat-eater, vegan, what?"

"There's the Mountain Oasis around the corner," Conway told her. "Tell them it's for me, they know what I like." He pulled a sticky pad out of his apron, scribbled down an address, and handed it to her. "You know where that is?"

The address read 215 Terrace Avenue #206. Bethany shook her head.

"It's about a hundred yards from your uncle Gerry's house. Big gray apartments, you can't miss 'em."

"He's not my uncle yet."

"And I pray to God he never is."

Going over to Conway's apartment felt like a *decision* in the dictionary sense of the word. Nolan had told her many times that it came from the Latin root for *cut,* and it seemed to her then that the beauty of life was in making clean decisions that shaped you completely. She would walk into the apartment as one person and leave it as another—as clean a cut as you could ask for. The woman at the sandwich counter, when she heard that half of Bethany's order was for Conway, smiled like she might have brought a sandwich or two over to his place herself. And it didn't matter—Bethany didn't want to possess him, she just wanted him to push her out of her too-tight skin and out of Nolan Purcell's universe.

Bethany felt bold until she walked up Terrace Avenue and saw her little orange rental car sitting by the curb across from Gerry's house. For a moment her legs wouldn't propel her any further up the street, and she dropped the sandwiches as if caught in her infidelity already. But there were too many trees in front of Gerry's house for Nolan to see her, even if he stood on the front deck with binoculars. She checked the apartment number on Conway's note and scurried around to the far side of the building, away from the street; she straightened her back as she headed up the stairs and rapped on his door three times fast. Underneath her sweat and shallow breathing lurked a calm new Bethany Bristol who held a knife above the vein that kept her life's blood flowing into Nolan.

Conway called out, "Just a minute!" but opened the door almost immediately. Bethany handed him the sandwiches, which he dropped onto a big stereo speaker. She walked to the middle of the living room and looked around—books everywhere, a bass guitar, a muddy mountain bike, a four-foot-long telescope, a cactus taller than she was covered with dried red flowers. Conway stood behind her, closing the door, and reached out to touch her left shoulder like he'd almost done in the bookstore when he thought she was Melanie. She let his fingers land this time, let his electricity sink into her skin until she couldn't tell it apart from her own. Then her right shoulder lifted up, aching for the same touch, and Conway put his other hand on it. Bethany turned around to face him and gripped his wrists.

"Touch me," he said, sliding his hands down to hers and bringing them to his face. Not a lot of people touched his face, she could tell. His skin softened almost in gratitude, then his hands ran back up her arms to her shoulders again.

"Did you like Melanie's shoulders?" Bethany asked.

"This isn't about Melanie."

"It'd be easier if it was. Don't you think?"

"No, I don't."

Conway picked her up and set her down on his hips; he was sturdy enough that Bethany could rest there without concern for her own balance. They kissed a lot more than she thought they would and didn't speak at all, not even to decide when to start undressing. She simply hopped down off of him and they stripped, laughing like teenagers about to race naked into the ocean. She reached between her legs and came up with two moist fingers, which she lifted to Conway's lips.

"I don't do that," he said, pulling his head back.

"Never?"

"No. Never."

"Okay then." Bethany crouched down to take him in her mouth awhile. He was already hard and didn't need further coaxing, but she wanted him to know that she wasn't a petty, tit-for-tat lover. That she gave it her all, didn't count favors. It felt great to fill her mouth up with something—her lying, hypocritical mouth that had said it loved Nolan so many times. She climbed onto Conway's hips again and slid him inside her.

"What's this about," Bethany asked once they settled, "if it's not my sister?"

"I'm doing the world a favor. Getting rid of two people's misery."

"Just one. There's nothing you can do about Nolan's."

"I wasn't thinking about Nolan's."

She had two strong orgasms, one shortly after they stopped talking and one later on, when Conway came. He warned her first and asked if it was okay, and when she said yes he didn't ask for details. He came hard, grunting like a weightlifter. Then they clutched each other until he hung her off him upside down, her hair grazing the floor and their bodies connected only at the hips and hands.

"I feel like a monkey," she said, letting out three little monkey hoots. It wasn't a particularly Bethany-like thing to do, but the old Bethany didn't really matter anymore.

"You kinda look like one, too."

"How long are you keeping me like this?"

"Until you pass out. Then I'll—I'll dress you up in circus clothes, or something."

"I'm game."

Conway waddled to the bedroom with Bethany hanging off of him and giggling. Then he set her on her back and ground against her slowly, with her hips lifted high, even though he was only half-hard. They kissed for a good ten minutes that way, until Bethany's back started hurting and she wriggled into a stretch. They lay face to face awhile, petting and rubbing bellies until Bethany broke the silence.

"You just changed my life." She was about to kiss Conway's nose until she remembered that she kissed Nolan there almost every day. So she kissed his eyelids instead.

"I hope so."

"Yes, you did." She turned away to roll her shoulders, to let the new Bethany start occupying her body. Wonderful midday light poured through a sliding door across the room. "Is that a balcony?"

"Yeah, one of my perks."

Bethany walked across the bedroom, threw open the door, and stepped onto the balcony completely naked. Below her was Terrace Avenue, and an unknown car passed by—she hoped its driver would recognize her, hoped its driver would stop at Gerry's house to report her infidelity to Nolan's family. But the car rounded the corner, oblivious, and Bethany deflated a little; she'd have to do the dirty work of confession herself. She stood awhile on the balcony to watch the street below, trying to glimpse Gerry's house through the trees and wanting the world to know that she'd become brand-new in another man's arms. Wanting all of Terrace Avenue to know, wanting Nolan to know, wanting at least their rental car—which she could see if she leaned out slightly over the balcony's railing—to know.

But the car didn't honk, didn't flash its lights in recognition. She and Conway showered and ate their sandwiches naked on his bed, chatting about Flagstaff and how it had changed since Bethany lived there. Chatting about how Melanie had started turning into a born again who wouldn't be amused to hear that her baby sister had slept with her ex-boyfriend on a whim. Eventually the conversation came around to how Bethany would break up with Nolan. She explained that it would be difficult because the condo was in her name even though he paid half of the mortgage.

"To hell with him," Conway said. "Kick him out and make him see who his friends are. Make him kiss some ass for a change."

"That sounds like a great idea." But already Bethany felt weak and remorseful, and wondered if she might just as easily cover the affair up. Simply keep it a secret inside her that she could hold over Nolan whenever he tried to hold something over her.

"You have to tell him." Conway took her arm and squeezed it. "If you don't tell him, I'm telling him. I'll get his number from Gerry."

"That's not fair."

"Neither is you not telling him. I don't want to see you hate yourself for this, and that's what'll happen if you don't tell him. I've seen it before, a million times."

"You mean with all the other women you've fucked during lunch break?"

"Okay, maybe a thousand times." He kissed her neck and looked at his clock.

"Going back to work?" Bethany licked stray mayonnaise from her fingers—another un-Bethanyesque behavior she suddenly didn't mind.

"Yep. Pictures first, though."

"Pictures?" She didn't know what to expect, but she let Conway hustle her into the living room and waited while he dug around for a nice 35mm camera and a tripod. He made her stand in the middle of the room while he composed a shot, then rushed in behind her while his timer counted down; he put his head on her left shoulder and swooped his arms down to her belly. Bethany smiled and cocked her head and lifted both arms, wove her hands together behind Conway's neck. Then the flash went off and he let her go.

"You do this with everybody?" she asked.

"There's not a lot of everybodies. But yes, I do."

"Always here? Always naked?"

"No, sometimes outside with clothes on. But this is right for you." Conway took two more pictures, put away his tripod, and started getting dressed. Bethany didn't. "You want to stay here awhile?"

"Sure. I won't take anything."

"You could, if you wanted to." His clothes went on fast, and soon he was at his door. Bethany stood in the middle of the living room as statuesquely as she could—she had a particular statue in mind, a bronze by Maillol that she'd seen at the Musée d'Orsay in Paris during one of her theater trips with Nolan. Conway came over and kissed her chastely, slowly, the way she believed that statues liked to be kissed.

"Just for the record—" He flashed his fingertips across the skin of her ribs. "I think we could love each other."

"Oh, I know that. It's very clear."

Then Conway was out the door and gone, probably forever unless she did something about it, and Bethany looked at her clothes strewn on the floor. They belonged there, she decided, at least for a while. She set the tripod up again and played with the camera until she figured out the auto shutter, then clicked off seven or eight pictures of herself laughing, dancing, singing. In the last shot she looked straight into the camera.

"Right now in this picture," she told the lens, "I'm saying I could love you."

Then the flash went off again. Bethany danced to the bathroom, wet her fingers on her tongue, and wrote the letter *B* on Conway's mirror. She ran back to the living room to get a business card from her wallet and tucked it into a corner of the mirror's frame, next to her signature. By the time she left the bathroom again, the letter she'd written on the glass — the claim she'd made on Michael Conway — was already dry and invisible.

VI.

At four o'clock Nolan called to tell Bethany that family business would keep him at Gerry's house until late. By then she'd stealthily picked up the car, driven around the foothills looking for Frank's cabin, slept, cried, bought a douche and thrown it away in the hotel Dumpster without using it, and twice tried calling Melanie to confess that she'd slept with Conway. At four-thirty she drove to North Flagstaff Dry Cleaning and learned, from its current owner, that Greg Purcell and Pete Conway had started it together thirty years ago. Six years and a few lawyers later, Greg sold it and left Pete with nothing. Two years after that, Pete drove off a cliff.

"There's two good brothers in that family, at least," the owner said. "One now, with Frankie gone. I hear Greg's kid went to Harvard on that money."

"Yale," Bethany corrected him.

The owner raised an eyebrow. "You married to him or something?"

"I was going to be." She showed him her hand, now empty of the engagement ring that she'd left in the car just to see how it felt to be single. She liked it and drove through town with her left hand out the window, advertising her freedom. By six-thirty Bethany felt guilty enough to put the ring back on and binge on French fries and ice cream at two different drive-throughs. At the hotel she tried to throw up but cried with her head against the toilet bowl instead, then jumped in the shower and rubbed her skin raw with a washcloth. She rubbed it raw again with a towel and curled up naked on the bed, testing out ways to tell Nolan that she'd slept with Conway, who by now felt less like a human being than a crime she committed long ago. Whatever way she imagined telling Nolan, the scene always ended with a theatrical slap to her face and her begging his forgiveness.

"That's bullshit," she berated herself. "You're brave with everybody but him."

Somewhere deep inside her, as Conway had said, she knew the truth and had the courage to speak it. After Nolan called at ten-thirty to say he was finally coming back to the hotel, Bethany stilled her body and narrowed her eyes to slits trying to find that courage buried in her flesh. She pictured herself with a flashlight, searching for it through a dark, soggy forest. But nothing leapt out at her from behind a tree, nothing strong and animalistic like she thought her courage would be, and soon the flashlight no longer cut through the darkness. Then it stopped working entirely. After that she put her face together as best she could, assumed that she would keep the Conway incident a secret for the rest of her life, and waited for Nolan.

"I'm sorry it took forever, babe," he said when he came through the door. Bethany sauntered over, naked and as kittenish as she could make herself, and he kissed her neck long enough to taste the sweat on it. "Shitty day. How was yours?"

"Fine. Went out and saw some things." She wrapped her arms

around him and rested her head on his chest. It felt thin and weak for a man's chest—barely able to support his own weight, let alone hers. "I missed you." She felt Conway across the room, shaking his head in disgust at her cowardice.

"Me too. My dad is fucking crazy." He took a deep whiff of her hair. "You smell nice." Nolan caressed the small of her back, then crashed backwards onto the bed. He slipped off his shoes and unbuckled his belt. "Lay down with me."

"No." Bethany stood as close as she could to the center of the room and tried to be a statue again. "Come get me."

"I want to feel your weight on me." Nolan grasped the waist of the imaginary Bethany who straddled him. "I want to feel your thighs."

"I want to try something different. Something new."

"Tonight?"

"Yes, tonight. We're in Flagstaff, honey. Let's make it mean something."

Nolan rolled out of bed and stood in front of Bethany, petting her as tenderly as he'd ever allowed himself. If she jumped on him like she'd jumped on Conway, they both would have crashed to the floor and hurt themselves, so instead she backed him up to the table where her suitcase sat open. She shoved the suitcase to the floor, spilling its contents everywhere, and pushed Nolan against the table.

"What are you doing?" He tried to grab her wrists and stop her.

"Everything. You don't have to do a thing."

She crouched down to take him in her mouth, though she didn't stay down half as long as with Conway. Once Nolan got hard enough she climbed onto him as best she could, one arm around his neck and the other against the wall for support.

"You like it?" she asked him.

"I'm really full. Be careful."

"Full like how?" Bethany kissed him so he couldn't answer right away. "Full enough so I could make you come just like *that?*"

She squeezed him down tight and he held his breath, holding back until she eased up on him. Nolan was absolutely scrupulous about never coming inside her without a condom, even when she had her period, and he pushed her off him—just jammed his hands between their thighs and shoved her away so hard she almost fell to the floor.

"We can't afford a baby right now," he said, tiptoeing over to the bathroom and fishing out a condom. "You said so yourself." After he put it on Bethany climbed onto him a little more recklessly than before, in a hurry to make him come. She bounced on him for a minute and he went wild, shouting and flailing his arm against the TV hard enough to move it.

"Better now?" Bethany said. Though she wanted to hang off him upside down to complete the homage to Conway, Nolan stood her up and kissed her hair, her ears, her neck. When she kissed his throat she remembered the smell of Conway's chest, and the truth-seeking flashlight that had died inside her found the courage she'd been looking for in the forest. She straightened her spine and reached up for Nolan's shoulders.

"Everything I just did to you?" she whispered.

"Yeah?" He looked sex-drunk, even a little bloodthirsty, like she'd finally become the whore he could never admit that he wanted her to be.

"Everything I just did to you, I did to Michael Conway this afternoon. I was on Terrace Avenue. I was a hundred yards away from you."

VII.

On the way to the airport they agreed that, since Bethany had destroyed the relationship, she would move out of the condo until Nolan found another place. Two hours after they got home, she took a few bags to her friend Alicia's apartment in Somerville. After feigning shock for half an hour, Alicia admitted that she found Nolan an absolute prick and hoped the breakup was for real. Bethany's sister, Melanie, to whom she confessed everything over the phone that night, wasn't quite as sympathetic.

"You could be pregnant," Melanie said. "You could have a disease."

"I accept that chance," Bethany told her.

"What do you mean, accept?"

"*Accept,* I mean *accept.* Is there something about the word you can't understand?"

On Monday at work she waited for a call or an e-mail from Conway — she'd given him her business card for this very reason, but worried that he'd gotten her home number from Gerry and called her there instead. Of course Nolan would withhold any messages to punish her, since he wasn't capable of anything but bitchy vindictiveness in situations like this. She imagined him inspecting his penis constantly, waiting for sores to grow on it now that he'd been infected by whatever gunk he imagined Conway having. It would serve him right if he got something, Bethany thought. Even more right if he never did, but spent the rest of his life worrying over it.

But nothing came from Conway on Monday. She went out for drinks with Alicia and told a couple more girlfriends about the fling, then went back to the office after hours to look at the Northern Arizona University website again. She couldn't find Conway at all this time, but blamed it on her mood. The things her sister said on the phone played repeatedly in her mind, twice as often and twice as loud because there was no mother left to say them to her. Just the born-again sister, doubling as the mother and making her feel like twice as much of a slut.

She went back to Alicia's and slept like a corpse, then woke up Tuesday feeling sick to her stomach. Pregnant for sure, she thought, and maybe worse. Maybe with a venereal disease that would attack her insides and destroy any hope of pregnancy for the rest of her life, or perhaps deform the baby already growing in her womb. But the sick feelings went away when she turned her mind to other things, like whether to change jobs and where to live next. Amherst, maybe, to get that Ph.D. It would be quite an accomplishment to get a Ph.D. as a single mother—people would find her formidable.

Flagstaff? No, not there. If she moved to Flagstaff it would look like she'd done it to be with Conway, and she had a policy against moving for a man's sake. She'd move there for the new start, maybe, without telling him beforehand. Move there to be in a place she'd felt at home in once, and might feel at home in again. But not for Conway, not for the man who was simply her doorway to freedom.

Bethany didn't feel sick on the jerky train ride downtown, or at her nine o'clock project meeting. But the nausea started again at ten-fifteen, when she walked back to her desk and saw a FedEx delivery man handing an envelope to the receptionist. Her company never used FedEx—they had a deal with UPS that all their clients took advantage of—so the package had to be from someone they didn't normally do business with. Bethany walked calmly back to her desk and waited three minutes, five minutes . . . After seven minutes she finally got a call about the package from the receptionist. Forty-five seconds later she was in the bathroom, sitting on the toilet with her slacks still on and reading a handwritten letter from Conway.

Dear Bethany:

I am overjoyed about what happened on Saturday. Hopefully it pushes you out of a miserable relationship and closer to your true self—I wish that for you even if I never see you again. But I remember that we talked about love, or at least used the word, so I want to tell you a little bit about the kind of love I believe in and want.

Somehow human beings come together from across millions of crossed signals and misdirected words, and manage to find the ones who make us feel fullest and holiest. The reason is simple: underneath all our language and civilization, we recognize the people we're supposed to reproduce with. If we have any humanity left in us at all, we listen to that voice and let it lead us to love. Love is about giving life, about creating more opportunities for joy and beauty in the world, and nothing would make me happier than knowing that the love we made will lead to new life.

In other words, I am praying every single moment that whatever birth control you may have used on Saturday utterly failed, and that you are pregnant with our child.

You are not the first woman who has made me pray for this —Melanie was another—and you may not be the last. Ever since we said goodbye I've been praying that I'll never need to make love with anyone else. That the last woman I made love to, Bethany Bristol, will be the only one for me forever. That this Bethany will grow our child inside her and come to live with me here, to raise that child in closeness and constant love the way children are meant to be raised.

I look back at the moment we had and pray that we seized it with enough passion to make it last. If that moment comes alive inside you, and if you will let it grow there—or if you want to seize moments like it again and again, until a child comes—then I am yours completely and forever.

> In love, respect, and hope,
> Michael Case Conway

P.S. There are two pictures in the envelope. One you will remember posing for, but the other you may not.

Bethany put everything back in the FedEx envelope and propped it against the toilet paper dispenser so she could pull down her slacks; she suddenly had the urge to pee. She'd heard that pregnant women needed to pee often and maybe she was one of them now. When she sat back down she took out the letter again, but couldn't comprehend a single word this time. Then she pulled the photographs from their thin, frosty 8 x 10 sleeve. The first one she recognized instantly—herself naked in the middle of the room with Conway behind her, his arms caressing her belly and her hands entwined around his neck.

They belonged together—their tawny skins, their dark curly hair, their sinews tough as the roots of desert trees. She looked at the Bethany in the picture and started crying because she was not that Bethany in real life. The woman in the picture was an animal of smells and tastes and movements, capable of giving life to the world the way Conway believed she could. The Bethany on the toilet seat was a shell, a fake, a lie. Nothing but a name on a report or a contract, or a condo deed she would gladly sign over to a man she had lied to for years.

Bethany moved on to the second picture, which showed her dancing and singing, and she smiled thinking how happy her surprise photos must have made Conway. In this one her eyes were closed, and her mouth rolled into an O that pointed upward to let a note fly toward the ceiling. She'd been singing something beautiful but indistinct when the shutter snapped—not a word but a pure note, and when she looked at the picture she felt that note floating up from her lungs again.

It was the hands and arms that really got her, though. She remembered the crazy dance she'd been doing, the way she threw her arms out wide whenever she shifted her weight from one foot to the other. But right then, when the camera caught her, she had her fingers woven together just below her ribs. Her arms, about to fly out in opposite directions with so much energy, made a perfect half-oval across her chest and belly. If there were a baby in the picture, with its back resting in her clasped hands, it would only need to turn its head to find her breast.

ACKNOWLEDGMENTS

I'd like to thank the following:

The Bread Loaf Writers' Conference, Middlebury College, and the LZ Francis Foundation for supporting emerging writers through the Bakeless Prizes.

Amy Hempel for picking this manuscript out of the pile and birthing two decades of wish into reality; Antonya Nelson and Lee K. Abbott for doing the same for individual stories within it.

Brandy Vickers, whose brilliant questions made this book better at every turn, and the rest of the team at Houghton Mifflin.

Ken Jacobs and Stan Brakhage, two filmmakers who taught me how to see.

Robert Olen Butler and Steve Katz, who showed me what it meant to walk the walk.

Charlie Mullen, Dianne Harrison, Linda Dittmar, and Suzanne Gluck for their encouragement at crucial junctures.

My Colorado writer friends for their camaraderie: David Mason, Robert Garner McBrearty, Laura Pritchett, Janis Hallowell, and Robert Root.

Family, blood and chosen: my wife, Jennifer, and sons, Lucas and Landon; my brother Tom; Joanne Grillo; the Cantors, Shernicks, Waltjes, Bayleses, and Yannacitos; Ernesto Acevedo-Muñoz and Jo-Ann Borys; Karol and Agnes.

My mother, Mary Ann, for always supporting my love of books.

My father, Tom, for all the typing that spilled up from the basement as you tried to put your life into words. May this book help bring you fruition and repose.

BREAD LOAF AND THE BAKELESS PRIZES

The Katharine Bakeless Nason Literary Publication Prizes were established in 1995 to expand the Bread Loaf Writers' Conference's commitment to the support of emerging writers. Endowed by the LZ Francis Foundation, the prizes commemorate Middlebury College patron Katharine Bakeless Nason and launch the publication career of a poet, a fiction writer, and a creative nonfiction writer annually. Winning manuscripts are chosen in an open national competition by a distinguished judge in each genre. Winners are published by Houghton Mifflin Company in Mariner paperback original.

2007 JUDGES

Amy Hempel   FICTION

Terry Tempest Williams   CREATIVE NONFICTION

Stanley Plumly   POETRY